MIRROR IMAGE

A MIKE PARSONS NOVEL

MALCOLM TANNER

Copyright © 2021 Malcolm Tanner
All cover art copyright © 2021 Malcolm Tanner
All Rights Reserved

This is a work of fiction. Names, places, characters and incidents are either the product of the author's imagination or are used fictitiously, and any resemblance to any actual persons, living or dead, businesses, organizations, events or locales is entirely coincidental.

No part of this book may be reproduced or transmitted in any form or by any means, electronic or mechanical, including photocopying, recording, or by any information storage and retrieval system, without permission in writing from the author.

Publishing Coordinator – Sharon Kizziah-Holmes
Cover Design – Jaycee DeLorenzo

Paperback-Press
an imprint of A & S Publishing
A & S Holmes, Inc.

ISBN 13: 978-1-956806-17-5

ACKNOWLEDGMENTS

Big thanks to my editor, Linda Knight. Linda always keeps my best interests at heart. She is a book warrior, and she knows what I like and don't like in my writing, but she knows how to suggest something new to me in the right way. The books don't happen without her much needed input.

Thanks to Sharon Kizziah-Holmes at Paperback Press for her assistance with formatting and interior design and to Jaycee De Lorenzo at Sweet and Spicy Designs for the amazing covers she has done for me over the years, including this one.

I thank my late parents, who both passed away over the past twelve months. Their loss has left a big hole in my heart. Thanks to them for their love, patience, and guidance that created a work ethic within me. There were times when plowing through this project was difficult during our mourning period, but I could always feel them pushing me on. That is what they would have wanted. I love and miss them both.

Finally, and certainly not the least, I thank my wonderful wife, Sandy, who has cheered me on through this whole process. She is my solid rock and whenever I feel challenged, she steps up and pushes me gently forward, giving me positive influence. I needed that to meet those challenges, especially this year. I don't know if I would have finished the project without her love and support.

Chapter 1

Perfect. Not many times was "perfect" used to describe a common business meeting. Sure, Paul had okay days and good days, but he would not use the word perfect to fit those days. Driving home from the meeting, Paul was feeling like his world was about to change. The presentation had gone well; he felt the interest and excitement among the business executives attending. He had looked good and had handled the questions and concerns like a pro. Paul was now thinking if Taylor's Brew House grew from ten to two-hundred-fifty franchises, he would be nearing life-changing money. Seventy-five million was money he could sink his teeth into. Now he just had to wait a few days to see if he had any bites. If he did, he would need to reel them in.

Paul believed the buzz flowing through his bloodstream came from the success of the meeting, not the alcohol he had consumed. Using a designated driver would not project the man he wanted the executives to see, so Paul got into his car and cranked the ignition. Besides, he was almost home; he would take his time getting there. Suddenly, he slammed on the brakes. Where in the hell did the sign come? *Detour? Since when?* He had come this way earlier in the day and now a sign read, "Road construction ahead". *Great! Simply great!* Paul backed his car in the nearest drive and turned around heading in the direction the sign pointed.

The road was unfamiliar to Paul. It was definitely darker as he drove away from the streetlights and onto a dirt road. Damn it! This car was his pride and joy and wasn't used to this type of terrain.

Suddenly, a bright light shone directly into his eyes, and he started to slam on his brakes, swerving to miss whatever was behind the light. It was too late. He hit something, a deer possibly. Getting out of the car and walking around the front, Paul saw he had hit a tree with his car. Damn country roads. He felt around the car for dents. He would just have to wait until he got home. Paul suddenly felt weak at the knees and knew he was going to be sick. As he bent over, blackness enveloped him.

Paul woke up the next morning with a doozy of a hangover. He couldn't read the numbers on the clock next to his bed. Stumbling to the bathroom, Paul tried to recall what happened the night before. His mind was fuzzy, and his mouth tasted sour. Looking in the mirror, Paul couldn't believe he had a black eye forming and a cut on his lip. His memory was starting to come back to him, and he hurried downstairs to check on his car. He was surprised to see the door leading into his garage wide open. He couldn't remember how he had gotten home or even to bed.

Rushing out, he let out a moan and a string of curse words. The fender of his new car was bashed in and the side mirror was hanging there. Paul remembered hitting something the night before... he checked around the entire car for further damages but didn't find anything outstanding except the trunk was not shut tight. As he opened the trunk, Paul leaned over and threw up all over the garage floor. It couldn't be! There was obviously a dead body lying in the trunk of his car. He quickly threw a blanket over the body.

He shut the trunk and found a shop towel to wipe his face. His head was throbbing. This could not be, and it could not have come at a worse time. He struggled with what to do. He thought of his fiancée, Trisha. He knew he was almost there in the business. His investors were about ready to buy in and this could not happen, not right now, not ever!

The floor, clean up the floor, Paul. He was on his knees scrubbing and then went around the side of the house to the faucet, filled a bucket with water, and brought it back into the garage. He finished cleaning and swept the residue out of the garage. Just when he had finished, Trisha opened the mudroom door leading to the two-car garage. "Paul, are you okay?"

"Yes, Trisha. I came outside to get some air. I had a rough night last night, but the meeting went great."

"Why don't you come inside and tell me about it?" she asked, waving her hand in a gesture beckoning him to her.

"I'll be right in."

Paul's world was spinning. He had to go somewhere to think, but he had to give Trisha some kind of excuse.

He knew Trisha would not be happy, but he quickly thought about showing her the car damage and saying he needed to go get an estimate. She could not see the car, as hers was nearest the door to the mudroom. It would be a good excuse to leave. Paul quickly decided calling the police was not an option, not at this moment. *I just can't, not after the last time I dealt with them over an incident in my bar. I never touched the woman, but they harassed me for months after she claimed it happened. What in the hell happened last night? I can't remember. Think, Paul, you have to remember. Your whole world depends on it.*

Paul went inside the house not realizing the trunk was not completely closed.

Chapter 2

Paul Taylor, a twenty-eight-year-old, entrepreneurial restaurateur, believed in success through old-fashioned hard work, leading him to be one of the state's latest and greatest figures in business. His long hours of developing a power-ridden concept catapulted him into the local scene as the next generation of young guns. The previous night's meeting with Silver Lake Equity Firm demonstrated Taylor's readiness for franchise growth, backed by the firm's prosperity and prestige. The well-earned ego of last night waned slightly with the alcohol-induced memory-lapse after he left the bar. He remembered questioning his sobriety. A nagging voice told him he should have played it safe. Something had happened. Something had gone dreadfully wrong. But with a body in his car, he had only the ending, not the increasingly grim events in between.

Paul was washing his hands in the sink, and Trisha was standing close by. He was nervous and shaky, not only from having too much to drink the night before but also from what he had seen in the trunk of the car. He had gotten up that morning and not seen Trisha in the bedroom. She had gotten up before him and sat out in the living area by the fireplace.

"So, how was the meeting last night?" Trisha asked, as Paul dried his hands on the kitchen towel.

"It went well. I think I have a solid equity firm, Silver Lake, interested in making the investment. If we close the deal, we're talking about the money we have been looking to have. They would sell the franchises, and we would negotiate the residual incomes from each place, then we would be set. If this goes well, then maybe we can feel secure in our future. Like, really secure. I just need to close the deal."

"Oh, how wonderful, Paul! We have been waiting for something like this to happen. With our future on track, we can think of getting married, building the house we dreamed of, maybe even having kids," she said, moving in closer to him and wrapping her arms around him, holding him close.

She stroked his back, and Paul suddenly felt the urge to hurl again, knowing something might keep his dreams from coming true. He had dated Trisha for four years now, and they had sacrificed the major things, so they could save for their wedding, the house, and all the finer things. He swallowed hard. "Yes, we're going to make it, and this deal is just the beginning."

Gently turning Trisha around to look at him, he took her hands and held them both as he looked deeply into her eyes. "We're going to be just fine." He wasn't so sure about what he just said, but he was sure about something else. He knew he had to make an excuse to leave. There was a dead body that needed to be disposed of in his car! He just didn't know how he was supposed to do that. Going to the police seemed like the right thing to do, but he was so close to his dream, and he and Trisha had planned for this all along. He couldn't have what he was working for all come crashing down. Not now.

Trisha looked closely at Paul's face. She reached up with her hand and gently stroked his cheek and said, "Paul, what on earth happened to your face? It looks like you have a black eye, and your lip is cut."

"I think it happened when I sideswiped a tree with my car last night. The fender is banged up. I'll have to take it to the body shop."

Trisha held his hand and started to walk to the bedroom. "I have something special to show you," she said, as she led him to the edge of the bed. "Wait here," she said in a sultry voice he had never heard her use before. She went into the bathroom and shut the door.

Paul was not really in the mood for games; he had a serious problem in his garage. Any other day he might have wanted to play along, but he couldn't reveal to Trisha about what was happening to him right now. He had major problems.

He went to his side of the sink and tried to brush away the vomit smell from his mouth. He could hear the shower running as Trisha stepped in. He finished brushing his teeth, gargled mouthwash, and went back to the bed and sat on the edge.

Suddenly, the door to the bathroom came open, and Trisha walked out in the finest lingerie he had ever seen. She started some sultry music drifting through the room. He swallowed hard and wondered what had made Trisha this aggressive. He had never seen this look in her eyes before. He did not hesitate as she pushed him back on the bed and quickly was on him before he knew it. Paul could not resist. They made love passionately. It was not only a sexual awakening for him, but also a mental relief from the scene he had witnessed in the garage. She fell asleep with her head lying on his chest. Paul felt her light and airy breathing. The sex was nothing like they had experienced before, and Paul lay there wondering where her sexual aggression had come.

However, there was a body in his trunk. A dead body mangled and bloody, the face unrecognizable. He felt as if he might be sick again, but he could not get up, not yet. He could not act as if something was urgent. He could not tell Trisha. *What am I going to do?*

The man, sitting in a distant car, watched Paul vomit in his garage and clean up the mess. He watched while Paul emptied the bucket of water on the garage floor. He sat in his car observing Paul's every move. Paul was too busy to notice he was there. He would have to wait for Paul to go inside, and when he did, the man would pull into the drive.

Having no neighbors for a square mile, Lee hoped he would not be noticed. This would be easier than he thought. When Paul had been inside for five minutes, he quietly pulled into the driveway. Paul had left the garage door open, so it made things even easier. He opened the trunk, wrapped the body in the blanket, and put it in the trunk of his own car. It went as planned, and now all he had to do was dispose of the body and watch Paul panic.

He knew Paul and was jealous of him from the very start. He had watched Paul grow his business, and he wanted to be like Paul. However, he was a minor, low-level competitor. Nevertheless, he would bring Paul Taylor down by making his life miserable. In fact, he could see Paul Taylor in jail. There is the ticket, Paul Taylor would be in jail, and he would be taking over

Paul's franchises. He had the plan, and this was just the start. Right now, he had Paul Taylor in a bad place.

The man drove off with the body. He hoped everything had gone well, and no one had seen him. He kept driving and knew exactly where he was heading. This would not be easy, but he had planned for quite some time, and his efforts would be rewarded soon. He just had to play it cool, and everything would be his.

With cruel eyes, he followed the road away from Paul's home. He had been in the area many times as a child, and he knew where he would go next. *I cannot wait to watch the guy go down in flames. Paul Taylor is the king of the restaurants, and Paul Taylor is so great! Ha! Paul Taylor is going to pay me or go to jail!*

CHAPTER 3

It had been a year in the making but the sign was finished, and the men were attaching it in front of their new building. Mike Parsons stood outside in the warm fall sun, watching the sign, M & M Private Investigators, go up on the building. He was proud, and he looked at his new wife, Katy O'Neal Parsons, and smiled. He thought back to all those times he and Katy, along with their friend, Andy Marx, had escaped the terror of Allison Branch. Marx had retired from the Milwaukee Police force and now their new office in a strip mall on Campbell Street in Springfield, Missouri, was open for business.

Andy and Katy both came outside to admire the sign with Mike. They all three smiled and high-fived and went back inside. The day was young, and they had lots of office furniture to arrange. It was a small office, but just right for the small business they wanted to have. Besides, people weren't impressed by your office but by your results, and Andy had a great job history.

"You know, Andy, this isn't going to be too bad. I like the sign, our location, and we've got the best ex-cop in the business as our lead investigator," Mike said, as he looked at Katy and winked. "Those sure were some crazy times."

"Hopefully, this work will never turn out to be that dangerous," Andy said. "Don't think we need any more suspense, for sure."

The three of them laughed and went back to work, moving file cabinets, desks, and chairs just how they wanted them to look. They were quiet and each of them had their own memories. Many of those memories did not go away, even in their sleep. Allison Branch lived in each of them, and in many ways, it would be hard to dispose of her memory. Andy and Mike had first met when Allison, Mike's police partner, had tried to kill them both. The case had taken them all over the United States and South America and involved a dangerous drug cartel. The thought of Allison gave Katy chills and reminded her of all her own weaknesses. She wanted to see herself as recovered and, for the most part, she was a much stronger person, having finished her paralegal studies and marrying Mike Parsons. He was what she needed, and she was the driving force behind his recovery.

Mike had re-applied for his attorney's license and, after his moments of fame with the Allison Branch case, the American Bar Association decided to grant him his license. In the past, Mike had given up his license and had gone into teaching law classes. He knew being an attorney was what he really wanted to do and was thankful the ABA saw that he was sincere. He wasn't having many nightmares any longer; he fought his battle long and hard. He was helping Katy with her insecurities, and she helped him win the battle of forgetting Allison Branch, and most of all, the evil of the cartel. He reminded himself every day was a new day, and his challenge of forgetting will be there for a long time. He took it one step at a time, and Katy was exactly the woman he needed. He reminded himself just how lucky he was.

Andy Marx had never married but getting back to Springfield was essential, as he needed to take care of his aging father. He didn't want to be a full-time cop in the city, but with his background, he knew he could be a private investigator. He asked for a waiver for the certification exam and was approved easily with past experience. He had to pay the $500 for his license and have proof of insurance, for at least $250,000.

Moving to this town was important and for Mike, getting his license in Missouri, was needed to make this organization work. Although they each had something to offer, it was just the beginning. They would see cases of cheating spouses, kidnapping, and even murder and missing persons come across their desk. The three of them each knew something about the seedy world and the terrible people inhabiting planet earth. They had seen it up close and personal. Each of them had much to offer, and now they just needed to advertise, get some phone calls, and get to work. It would not be long until they got their first job.

M&M was now in business, and the three of them were about ready to break for lunch. They locked their office and headed over to Taylor's Brew House in Redfield for some specialty burgers and a lunch beer. Since they moved here, it had become one of their favorite hangouts.

Lee Hamlin drove faster as memories began to flood his mind. He was the son of Elmer and Grace Hamlin. He had grown up physically abused by an alcoholic father. Jobs were hard for his dad to keep, and alcohol was an easy fix for his father. His mother didn't work outside the home and the debt grew month by month. His father and mother fostered a second child for money and that paid off some debt. They never really wanted to be parents. The children were good candidates for removal by the Family Services Division. It was never to be, as the mother, Grace Hamlin, stayed sober enough to keep fooling the authorities and keep the children.

He arrived at the old farmhouse he had used on occasion after his drunken father died. He never missed the old bastard. He had taken a few severe beatings from him, and he was not sorry to see him die. In fact, he had wished for his father's slow death, and his wish came true when Elmer Hamlin died a painful death from lung cancer.

Lee sat in the car knowing what he must do and drove around back to where the freezer was—empty and still plugged in. He stepped out of the car, looked at the old house, and shook his head. He could not rent it out again. It would have to stay empty for a while. He opened the trunk and saw the blanket with the body underneath. He hoisted it up over his shoulder, raised the lid of the freezer, and put the body inside with the few rolls of hamburger left by the last tenants. He shut the lid and threw the blanket in the pile of trash to burn. He then grabbed the duffle bag from inside his car, walked up on the porch, unlocked the door, and went inside the house.

Since the last tenants left, the old house had been abandoned. The smell was dank and damp, and he needed to open some windows. The fresh air was welcome inside, and he headed to the bathroom to strip off his clothes and shower. After drying off, he took bleach wipes and cleaned all of the handles and doorknobs in the house, put the towel back in his duffle, and carried his clothes out back to the burn pile. He wiped the handles to the freezer, and he took out his lighter and set the clothes on fire. When it was burning hot, he threw on the blanket and his shower towel. He waited around to make sure all of the clothes burned completely.

Lee went back into the house and studied his old environment one last time. He could picture the memories of the beatings. He could see the Family Services people who sat in this very living room. He could even hear his mother, crying from the other room, when his father had not returned home from drinking, probably sleeping around with some town whore. He shook his head and tried to relieve himself of those cold, dark memories, the ones scarring him for life. He was turning into what his father said he would be—a no-good son-of-a-bitch.

CHAPTER 4

Dan Taylor, Paul's dad, was an ex-Marine. He was a standout athlete at his high school, and he skipped a college scholarship offer to serve in the United States Marine Corps in Vietnam. He earned the rank of lieutenant and commanded men on the ground. He had been through much in his stint in the Vietnam conflict and his son, Paul, had always wanted to follow his dad's example and be a Marine as well. His father discouraged going into the military, and Paul went on to college at Missouri University, earning his business degree. His dad would tell him many times, the memories he thought he had left behind in a cruel world of war would always haunt him. He always told Paul he was just trying to protect his son from having that kind of mental anguish.

Paul was disappointed that he couldn't follow in his father's footsteps, but with his college business degree, he set out to open his very first restaurant and bar in the spring of 2016. He studied the concept he had for a place of his own, while he worked in a nightclub where he made several contacts. He asked questions, worked hard, and, above all, saved money like crazy trying to fund his first project. When he had enough money and connections, he and his partners opened their first place on their own.

Dan was proud of Paul, and he wanted his son to have success. Even though Dan was retired from the military on a pension, he did offer Paul money to get started. Paul refused, wanting to make it on his own, something which his dad would be proud. Paul did get it done, and Dan was immensely proud.

Dan's world was good at this moment. He had a son who was achieving much at a young age. Dan had a comfortable income, but the one thing he did not have was a wife. He lost her in a car accident when Paul was just fourteen years old. Dan continued to raise Paul through the difficult teen years on his own. He never did find another wife. He loved Rebecca too much, and there would be no one to take her place. Dan knew this for sure. Every time he looked at his son, he always saw Rebecca's face. They looked so much alike. Paul could always stir Rebecca's memory for Dan.

He finished his dinner and went out on the deck outside his home. It was a small home, in a comfortable neighborhood. He could afford more, but since it was just him, his small, three-bedroom and two-bath place suited him just fine. He sat in the rocker with a cigar and a glass of scotch, just being quiet and listening to the birds chirping. He took a large drag off his cigar and blew the smoke skyward, watching the smoke dissipate into the cool fall air. He wished when the smoke cleared, the real Rebecca would appear. Of course, she never did.

Paul got up from the bed and went to shower. Trisha was still asleep, and Paul had rehashed in his mind how Trisha was so intense in her lovemaking. He wasn't going to complain about the sex. He just saw something different in her sexual behavior. He finished showering, and he knew he had some things to get done. There's a body in his car. The car fender is dented and beat to hell. His tongue touched the cut on his lip but couldn't remember how he had gotten it.

He dried off, stood in front of the mirror, and noticed his black eye. It wasn't too bad, but it was noticeable. He struggled to remember who hit him or was it the wreck? He couldn't remember what had happened. He quietly dressed as Trisha began to wake up, he was almost finished and picked up his car keys from the dresser and leaned over to kiss her goodbye.

Her fragrance was captivating, and he was wishing none of this would have ever happened, and he didn't have to leave. However, he had a body in the trunk and dents in his car. He had to do something about the body, and the stark reality of what might have happened made him start to sweat again.

"Love you."

"Love you, too." Trisha said, as she sat up exposing her naked breasts.

"I'll be back soon."

Katy, Mike, and Andy sat at the four-top table at the restaurant reminiscing over their past escapades and discussing their future. Mike and Katy had married the year before in a quiet ceremony in Milwaukee. They did not have children but having them was not totally out of the realm of possibility, although Mike was getting up in age for raising kids. Katy was still hopeful Mike would come around soon. Marx's retirement party from the police department in Milwaukee was a big deal, and Mike and Katy were both happy for him, but this move to Springfield had not been what they had thought of until Andy's dad needed care. They felt like they wanted to do this private investigator thing and, since their ties were no longer in Milwaukee, a change of scenery would do them all good and give them a fresh start.

Mike still had dreams of firing the fatal shot killing Allison Branch. He never could decide who killed her, Andy or him. However, the police report said Andy fired the shot. It was less complicated that way. However, in his mind, Mike Parsons thought he did kill Allison. The dreams had slowed down now, and life was getting back to normal. The three of them, investing in this company, would soon have their first case. Then, the team would be on their way to doing what they liked, solving mysteries.

"Hey, anyone want to guess what the first case is going to be?" Andy Marx asked.

"I'll say dead beat dad not paying child support and skipping town," Katy said.

"I'll take a cheating husband, probably the most common," Andy said.

"I'll take the coolest missing person's case ever. So hard, it takes two years to solve it," Mike said, taking a sip of his cold beer. "But, please, no murder at first. We have to ease back into this thing."

They shook their heads in agreement, as they enjoyed the rest of their lunch. Andy looked out the window and thought, *Yes, please, no murders. I was shot once before, and I'm not looking to be shot again. It's why I retired.*

"Andy... Andy, you're not eating," Katy pointed out,

bringing Andy back to reality.

"I'm sorry, guys; I guess I was just daydreaming a bit. So, what more do we need to do at the office?"

They finished and Mike grabbed the check. They got in the car and headed back to their new office on Campbell Street. The workmen had finished installing the sign, and M&M looked almost ready for business. Now all they would need is some work. They had bills to pay.

Chapter 5

Paul was in his garage and worried about what he had to do. He had just left Trisha naked and lovely, to go back to his nightmare of a dead woman's body in the trunk of his car. He took one more look at the dented fender of his car and then pulled out his phone to take a few pictures. He didn't know if he had the guts to photograph the body, but he had to look just one more time, if he could keep from heaving again. Paul opened the trunk, and his heart skipped a beat. The body was gone.

He swallowed hard, and he thought he must be going crazy. *It was there, I saw it. Am I going crazy? There was a damn dead body in my car. Now nothing? What's wrong with my memory, why can't I remember? Maybe I was still hung over, and there wasn't a body. I just couldn't remember. Obviously, I blacked out, and drinking is causing these problems. I need to straighten myself out.*

Paul quickly went outside and looked around,

thinking he might find someone or something out there, but there was nothing. He was panicking and went back inside the garage. He started to sweat again. Just then, Trisha appeared at the door leading from their kitchen to the garage.

"Paul, are you okay out here?" she asked, standing there with no top. "And, Paul, please don't be long," she said, as she turned with a sexy smile and went back inside. Any other time, Paul would have welcomed the invitation. Right now, he was battling some sort of demon.

Paul got in his car, leaving the garage quickly, hoping Trisha would not notice how bad the dents were. He drove the car out on an unpaved country road close by. He figured he could find his way back to the spot where his wreck occurred... a deserted spot where he hit the tree. He found a place, seemingly abandoned, and pulled into the drive. Paul tried to find the detour sign on the road. He thought it had to be close to where he was, but he didn't see it.

Paul got back in his car. He couldn't help but feel he was being watched, but he quickly put the thought out of his head. He slowly dropped his head and rested it on the steering wheel. He began to cry. He knew something was wrong, but what was he supposed to do?

He told himself he had worked hard to achieve his goals, and the life he and Trisha had dreamed of waited just around the corner. His tears were real, he knew he had seen a body and not going to the police was wrong, but what body? The opportunity to franchise was the most important decision in his life. If he could just get by this, things would be back on track. His curiosity began to escalate as he drove back to the city. *Someone is out there with a dead body, or was there? I can't believe if I had hit someone,* I *wouldn't have stopped or tried to help. Did I do something and blacked out on my feet?*

Paul reached up with his hand and ran his fingers across the cut on his lip. He then felt the shiner on his eye. He knew he didn't hit himself. Something was wrong and it was going to drive him crazy. There was a crash, a dead body in the trunk, dents in my car, a black eye, and a cut lip. *What in the hell had happened? Did I just dream it all? No accident scene, no body, and the cops would think I was crazy.* Paul drove on to the road he was on last night, looking for a scraped up tree, but it wasn't there.

Andy Marx was sitting at his desk. The thoughts of Allison Branch, and all she tried to do to kill him, came flooding back. He was shot and damn near died, chased her and her cronies all over the world. He recalled the chase scenes as if they were yesterday, and it gave him chills. He guessed she tried killing him two or three times, but somehow, he survived. And, now, after retirement, he had a much simpler life. Now, he just waited for the call to help someone find a missing husband, a missing person, or perhaps a good cold case. It was much easier work and less risky than before. At least it was what he wished.

The phone rang and Katy answered, "M & M Private Investigators."

The woman's voice on the other end was requesting help in finding a dead-beat husband who had run out on her and her two kids. Her dad was willing to pay the fees if they could find the guy.

Katy took notes and then said she would transfer the call to Andy Marx, the investigator. Andy took the call, while Mike was busy sorting papers on his desk. Mike listened half-heartedly to what was going on, but it seemed like the type of cases they were going to get. It was fine that this type would be more than enough to fill their day, excitement wasn't the issue, but investigations and the law were.

"We'll be glad to take the case. We ask for a retainer fee of $250. We usually work for $70 an hour plus expenses until the case is complete. We've got a legal guy in the office who works for a bit higher fee if you need some type of defense or, in your case, you want to sue," Marx said.

The woman agreed and said she would have her father come by and sign all the paperwork and agreements. Marx agreed and sent her back to Katy to set up the appointment for tomorrow.

M & M Private Investigators was now officially in business. The three of them were back in business, doing what they liked to do.

"Well, case number one is on the way. She will be here tomorrow to sign the papers," Marx said, as he looked over at Mike. "You get the papers ready for her to sign and we all three have participated in case number one. We will have more to do beginning tomorrow, but for now, let's celebrate!" he exclaimed, as he walked over to their new office kitchen and opened the door to pull out the new bottle of Dom Perignon he had bought for this very occasion. He got some champagne glasses and put them on the lunch table. He poured each a small glass and raised his for the toast. "To M & M Private Investigators, may we always stay safe, work hard, and, most of all, prosper."

The three of them toasted their glasses together and downed the bubbly concoction. Katy looked at Mike and smiled. He returned the smile. The three of them began to talk of what they needed to do to get started on case number one. There would be many more. Case number two would be the one they would long remember. They just didn't know it yet.

CHAPTER 6

Trisha had known as long as she could remember that she was adopted, and her adoptive parents were good about telling her what they did know, but it seemed like a mystery as to who the biological mother was. Trisha just wanted, like most adopted children, to know her heritage. Her parents, Rich and Carol Dishman, were good people and loving to her. They raised her well and were excited when she announced Paul and she were thinking of getting married. They loved Paul, and they were so impressed with his ability to take care of Trisha. They felt comfortable knowing good things lay ahead for her.

Trisha had always wanted to know about her birthparents and wondered if she had any relatives. She thought about using one of the DNA searching companies to do some background on her family. A few months ago, she had gotten the packet and sent the information to begin the process. Trisha may not have found out the answer to her past, but she always wanted to know, so it was worth a try. It had only been two weeks ago, so she thought it may arrive any day. She waited patiently.

Lee Hamlin was driving back to his apartment in Springfield. He had business items to take care of, and he thought he had done everything exactly right in taking care of the body. Now, it was time to plan some harassment.

Lee had always hated Paul Taylor. Paul played ahead of him on the basketball team. Paul had a top-class ranking, and Paul always had his girlfriend, the one Lee coveted. Lee was always in detention, but Paul was never in trouble.

Paul is still the guy ahead of him, getting all the recognition in the local papers and local chambers where he had restaurants. He was often the speaker, and Lee had not been invited once to lead a meeting or seminar although they were in the same field. Now he was going to fix this problem. He had already started. He would bring Paul Taylor to his knees. Lee did have a few notes to make first.

He needed to play with Paul's mind a bit, just to make him understand someone knows and someone is watching. It would be just the right amount of torture without giving everything away. He hoped eventually to force Paul to turn himself into the police. He knew if his plan worked, Paul Taylor would not be around to get in his way again. Ever. Lee knew where the body was located. Paul did not even know if there really was a body. Lee laughed to himself.

Lee went inside his apartment and grabbed some blank paper, magazines, and glue. He put on rubber gloves and began to make his first message. He cut letters carefully, laid them on the sheets of paper, and began to make short, cryptic messages.

Hours later, when he had finished three of them, he carefully folded each one, put them in envelopes, careful not to lick or seal them. He placed each blank envelope on the table, proud of what he had just accomplished. He had thought long and hard on how to get at Paul Taylor, and now, he had the perfect way to drive the asshole crazy and put him behind bars for good. Lee Hamlin smiled.

He stuffed the first note in his jacket pocket and headed to the car. Lee planned to place the first note today. He had somewhere to go, but first he had a call to make. After that, he would track down Paul. If Paul wasn't around, he would find another way to deliver the note, but he would deliver it today. He knew Paul's office location, and he would go by before heading to his own business.

Trisha walked around her large empty house in her robe. She sat in the large screened-in sitting room, sipping her coffee. She had dreamed of this life many times, a large home, a handsome man, and maybe a family of her own. She smiled as she looked out the window, living contently in the moment. She took a deep breath and began to recall all the things happening for her to be here with Paul Taylor. Life was good right now. Life was particularly good.

Paul called his body shop friend, Matt, and told him he really needed to get some dents fixed. He stopped at his office parking lot before taking it in and looked again at the damage. He found it odd looking, as if someone had beaten it with a sledgehammer. He studied it for a moment. He felt a bit more at ease, thinking maybe he did have a way out, maybe no one would know, and the body was nothing for him to be concerned about. He must have imagined the body as a form of just not being sober, possibly a hallucination. He went inside to check his email before heading to Matt's Auto Body Shop in Redfield.

Lee almost drove away, until he caught sight of Paul's vehicle turning into the parking lot at Taylor's Brew House offices. Lee parked across the street and observed. He saw Paul looking again at the dents in the side. Lee knew how they got there; Paul did not. Lee took out his phone and took a few pictures. Never have quite enough evidence. He watched Paul walk inside the building and thought it might be the right moment to place the note, but he thought better of it, knowing Paul probably had cameras hung on the building.

Lee saw Paul walk back out and get in his car. He followed at a safe distance as Paul's car was heading back into town. He followed all the way to Matt's Auto Body and waited. Paul went inside the shop and left the car outside. Lee sat in silence waiting for Paul to return. Another car drove up and Paul got in; it appeared to be a rental car as Paul got in and drove off. Lee waited until Paul had a few seconds driving away. *Damn him, I'll get the note placed or else.*

Lee drove a half mile from Matt's Auto Body, put on his rubber gloves, ball cap, and sunglasses, and started to walk along the sidewalk. Lee figured out that Matt probably had cameras around his garage. He kept his head down and his eye on Paul's car. He was pleased when he got to the parking lot and saw the car parked far from the building. He started walking quickly to the car, hoping to stay out of sight. He stopped as someone came out of the office door, heading to Paul's car. Suddenly, they turned around and went back into the office. He had to be quick. He carefully placed the note under the windshield wiper and walked back to his car and left. The first part of the plan was in action.

Marx set out to track down the deadbeat dad the next day. The father of the distressed woman came in to pay the retainer, and Marx already had some information. The wife, with the child support needs, provided the remaining information. Marx said he thought he could easily do this in a few days, waved goodbye to Katy, and was out the door.

Katy went over and pulled a chair up to Mike's desk as he was looking over the paperwork signed by his first case. Mike looked up from his papers.

"Hey, there's my favorite bartender!" he exclaimed, as he reached across the table and held out his hands.

"And there's my handsome, attorney customer," she said, as she took his hands in hers.

"I should now say, my favorite paralegal," he said, with a grin. "I think back to those days and how we luckily got together. I have to wonder about myself. I was so lost at times."

"Ah, but aren't you glad I never gave up?" Katy asked.

"Oh, yes, I don't know where I would be right now without you, dear Katy."

Mike got up and went around to the other side of the desk and rubbed Katy's shoulders, then reached down and kissed her on the cheek.

"You, my dear," he said, "were meant for me."

Katy smiled and thought to herself what had brought them together.

It was a crazy ride, me getting Mike Parsons to look at me differently besides being his favorite bartender. I knew he had something there for me, but I could never figure out why he would never commit. Then, there was the evil of Allison Branch. I could never figure out how someone could be so vicious? How did we survive?

The thoughts sent shivers down her spine as she remembered the pain and the suffering at the hands of Allison Branch. It was a wonder they were even alive today. Katy, deciding to put it away for now, stood up and faced Mike. She was stronger now and had gained much more confidence with herself.

"I love what we're doing, and I hope our business is a success. But we will not have to live through another Allison Branch case, will we?"

"These things are easily handled by Marx in the field, and we do the legal stuff here. So, rest easy, my dear. I think this will be a much smoother life. Besides, I think Andy misses a little action. Everything we do here is the simple stuff."

"Promise me something?" she asked, putting her palms against the side of his face.

"Anything, for you."

"Don't get mixed up with anyone so crazy again. Not if you can help it. Please let Andy do the dangerous work. I don't think I can go through it again."

Mike smiled, held her close, and whispered softly in her ear, "I'll do my best."

They ended their embrace and went back to filing all the paperwork on the first case. Katy thought to herself. *I'll do my best. I'm not sure he believes in what he just said. In some ways, I think he misses the excitement, too.*

Katy could not let go of his words. He only said he would do his best, but he did not promise. For Katy, she just knew she could not lose Mike and the only thing she thought of was the phrase at their wedding, "until death do you part."

She quickly shook the thought from her head and began to finish the work. She had no idea this work could lead into something much more dangerous than filing papers. She had her fingers crossed, hoping it was all she and Mike would have to do.

Sometimes, though, crossing your fingers is not enough.

CHAPTER 7

Marx had easily found the whereabouts of the deadbeat dad. He found a lead from a car dealer who sold the man a $2,000 white Chevy Cruz. He said the guy was in a hurry and matched the description of the picture Andy had shown him. He paid in cash.

Marx next went to run the VIN number and found all the recent local licensures through a cop friend of his at the Springfield DMV. He found the white vehicle registered to an Alex Roberts of Springfield, MO. The address was 2244 W. Tracksell, Apartment 2.

On the way to the address, Marx thought of all the crazy stakeouts and investigations of Allison Branch. This reminded him of staking out Mike's old apartment complex. It reminded him of the evil Allison Branch, too. She was a match for him. His old partner, on the Milwaukee Police Force, went crazy, and he never knew her until she snapped. He should have been more perceptive about her, seen the rage, and should have recognized what was going on. She hid it so well. She seemed quite normal to him for the most part, and he liked her competitiveness on the streets. He just didn't know how crazy she was and how she was a ticking time bomb ready to go off. He didn't realize how deeply she was tied into the dirty money of a drug cartel. You just never know someone like you think you do.

Marx stopped his car in front of unit 2, shook off the thoughts of being restrained, shot and almost killed by his female ex-partner. He even wondered if she was dead. He knew she was, but he just couldn't quit seeing the gun pointed at him with her angry face screaming at him, shooting him twice, the blood flowing and thinking he was about to leave this world. He stopped the thoughts the best he could and continued to watch the apartment. He was looking for Alex Roberts, the alleged deadbeat dad. His car was there, so Andy suspected he was at home.

A few minutes later, Marx saw a guy heading into the house. He double checked the picture and made sure he had the right guy. He made a phone call.

"Hello," the woman's voice on the other end said.

"Yeah, this is Marx. I found your guy. I have a few photos I took, and he's not alone. He has a woman with him. No doubt, I thought you might want to know. Now the next thing you can do is contact my partner, Mike Parsons, at the firm, and he can draw up legal papers for enforcement. Your ex can run from me, but he cannot hide. I will always find him, and he's better off paying you what he owes. I will confront the guy. He can be a good boy and pay what he owes, or he can pay heavy fines or even go to jail if he likes."

"Thanks, Mr. Marx," the woman said. "I really appreciate this."

"No problem. Your money spent will be well worth it."

Marx hung up and got out of his car. He went to knock on the door. A woman, scantily dressed, answered and yelled, "Hey, Alex, some guy for you." She let Andy inside.

He handed his card to Alex. "Mr. Roberts, I'm Andy Marx, a private investigator from here in Springfield. You can run from me, but you can't hide from me. You seem to have an obligation to the former Mrs. Roberts to pay your support. I suggest you do it before you run out of time. You were easy to find this time, and you will be found wherever you choose to run. I guarantee you. I'm good at what I do." Marx turned to the woman, "Goodbye, ma'am."

Andy walked back out to his car and felt satisfied the subject would not leave. He waited for an hour, just in case. His first case had been a simple one. He picked up the phone to call Mike and give him the particulars and a heads-up that the ex-wife would be coming in soon to draw up papers. Case number one was in the books.

Paul heard his phone ring and answered immediately. His friend, Matt, was on the other end.

"Hey, Paul, you need to come by. There was a note left on your windshield after you left. I found it when I pulled the car inside."

Well, what does it say, Matt?" Paul asked.

"Well, let's just say you better get down here. I'm the only one who has seen it, and it's not really something you should talk about on the phone."

"I'm at the restaurant; I'll be over in just a second."

Paul hung up and had a few last-minute details for the manager before he went out to his rental car and left for the body shop. He felt a knot begin to form in the pit of his stomach. He knew something bad was in the note. His mind began to shuffle the events of a couple of nights back: the blinding light, cut lip, black eye. What exactly had happened? He found a body in the trunk of his car. It was real and it was there. Unless he was crazy, he knew it was there. Now the body was gone, the evidence was gone, and surely, no one could pin this on him. The note, what does the note say? Paul was driving faster as his thoughts were moving at lightning speed. He had to see the note and what was written on it. It would mean someone else knew and the someone else was Matt, his friend. Could he explain this to Matt or was it better to keep him out of this, pretending it was some crackpot thing?

Paul was breathing hard when he arrived at the body shop. He had to calm down.

You must calm down, right now. You cannot show Matt any fear. You cannot make up a story you don't know or can't explain in any reasonable way. Just tell Matt it is a crazy person trying to bring me down. Relax, breathe easy, and do not let on to Matt you know anything about this.

Paul got out of his car and walked in. Matt saw him across the office and waved him into the back. Paul went inside Matt's office and sat across from Matt's desk. Matt turned over the note, which was face down on the desk. He handed the note to Paul, and Paul read the note with letters affixed to a blank page. The note read, **I know what you did and I think you are missing something.** Paul stared at the note and calmly looked up at Matt and said, "Probably this is just someone trying to intimidate me and play some kind of prank."

"Maybe, but maybe you should call the cops," Matt said, looking concerned.

"Aww, I just think it's some crackpot thinking he's funny. Look, I'll keep this, but I don't think it's really anything to worry about. How's my car?"

"We just got started," Matt replied. "We should have it done by tomorrow, if that's okay."

"Sure, sure, Matt, it's okay," Paul said, looking at the note still. *Yeah, whoever wrote this knows the something I am missing is a dead body. Or am I? Maybe, I should ask my dad what to do? He would give me good advice. I have worked so hard to get to this point in the business. This just cannot happen now.* He had a few more things to do before going home to Trisha.

"Paul... Paul, are you okay?" Matt asked, startling Paul just a little.

"Yes, Matt, I'm fine. I'll just take the note with me. It's probably nothing."

"Listen, you be careful, friend. You go to the cops if you need to."

"Sure, sure thing, Matt. Thanks again for fixing the car for me. Call me when you get done."

They shook hands and Paul left, carrying a much bigger load on his shoulders than he had when he came in. He hurried on to his rental and started the engine. He headed back to the restaurant as he had a few things to do. He loved Trisha, and he did not have the nerve to tell her about this. Was this the right time, or should he talk to his dad first? He was torn about what to do and the events slowly happening to him were starting to become a mental burden, one he did not need as he was about to make the deal of a lifetime.

He could not concentrate on his work, and he told his manager he had to go home for a while. He got into the car and read the note once more. *I know what you did. I think you are missing something. It must be why the body was gone. Someone took it. Who? Why? Where is it? Is there a body?*

Paul headed home, and he was facing a dilemma.

Talk to Trisha or not? It is the main question. He debated all the way home, going back and forth with decisions. He would debate for some time longer.

CHAPTER 8

It had been two days since Andy had finished the deadbeat dad case, and there were two more cases on the burner when he arrived the next day. They seemed easy to him, and he began to think he might be missing the old cop work he had done before. He didn't miss the dangerous parts, but he did miss the investigative part. He wanted to go back and put the pieces together of crimes, but he did feel he had a safety net with this job, and it allowed him much more peace of mind. However, like all those retired from their former jobs, going back in your mind to those workdays was something occurring daily until you grew accustomed to retirement. Andy shook it off and thought this notion would soon go away.

He entered M & M Private Investigators and met Mike and Katy in the office. He grabbed a cup, poured a coffee, and sat at his desk.

"The first case was easy. Have you got something tougher for an ex-cop to do?" Andy asked.

"Just got a new case last night. Needs some information gathering and investigating, but it is interesting. Seems like a grandfather decided to kidnap his own grandkid. Mother said grandpa didn't think the guy she was with was worth a damn, so he took the kid. Of course, the mom is furious, but there may be a good reason he took the kid," Mike said.

Katy interrupted, "Yes, but sometimes, it could be a dementia thing which could put the child in danger."

"Yeah, if you have a file started, I'll take a look at it."

Katy walked over and laid the file down on Andy's desk. She remembered at one time, she had given up on Mike, and Andy was someone she had an interest in. It was long ago, and she quickly dismissed the thought. She had Mike now, and they were working on having a child. A family was something Katy had always wanted, and she desperately wanted to become a mom with Mike. She had been frustrated lately, not getting pregnant, but she was going to keep trying, and, surely, it would happen.

Marx was writing things down and making a few calls to get more information on vehicles, plates, and descriptions. He browsed the photos of the kid and the grandpa. He found it sad, and he assumed in his own mind it was the reason he never married. Family caused too many complications. His own parents and siblings had given him a great childhood, but he never trusted himself to be a parent. Much less a good one like his own parents. Cop work just wasn't for a family. He had made it to forty without a wife, and he guessed he didn't need one now. He looked up from his work and at his partners. They were busily typing and reading files when he broke the silence.

"You know, I hate to bring this up, but don't you wish just a little, and just at times, mind you, we had a villain to chase once more? I mean, I don't want to bring back the old memories, but if something a bit more exciting doesn't come along, I may have to come out of retirement," Marx said, only half smiling.

"I don't know," Mike said. "I don't think either Katy or I could endure the pressure one more time. To me, the simple stuff is good, right now."

"I get it, but sometimes I miss the thrill of the chase, the hunt, the guessing games, and the gut feelings. You were good with those, Mike."

Katy felt a chill go down her spine. The men talked on, and she remembered Allison's face, her smell, and her penchant for evil. Katy had been bound, drugged, and beaten at the hands of Allison Branch and why in God's name she had come into this conversation was beyond Katy at this point. She stared off into the distance. Her thoughts went back to the awful experiences...

"Katy... Katy, are you okay?" Mike asked, as he saw the blank look on his wife's face.

"Yes, Mike, I'm fine. You know, I was just thinking about, about, well, Her."

"Well, don't," Mike said, looking into her eyes. "She's gone now; she can't hurt us any longer. We'll change the subject."

They all three quietly went back to work. They knew that someday they might have to face another villain. For Katy, facing another villain was the very last thing she wanted to do.

Paul Taylor had a decision to make. Should he show this note to Trisha or should he take the note over and tell his dad what happened? His dad was a straight up guy, and he would probably want to call the police. Paul trusted his dad to do the right thing. Could his dad be convinced just to help him investigate what was going on?

He was almost home, and he had to decide. He turned the car around in the parking lot of the local grocery store, got back on Highway 13, and headed to Dan Taylor's house. He felt he could not tell Trisha yet, and it was something he had to keep quiet. Paul knew his dad would encourage him to tell his bride-to-be, but Paul needed his dad to be with him on this one. There was so much at stake and if the equity company's decision to move forward with his restaurants came through, Paul would be a major player in this business for a long time. Security and success, and lots of it, were coming his way. *Who is trying to stop me?*

He pulled into the drive of his father's house, hoping his dad would be home. He parked the car and grabbed the note lying on the seat. He went to the front door where his dad, Dan Taylor, was there to open the door for him. Paul stepped inside, went to the living room, where they sat in chairs opposite each other. Paul held the paper in his hand and after the customary "how are you" exchanges, Dan noticed his son's hand was shaking, holding a piece of paper in his hand.

"Son, what's wrong? Your hand is shaking. What is the paper you are holding?"

"Dad, listen, I know what I'm about to tell you seems way out there, but just listen before you break in. Something bad is happening to me, and I can't explain it. Now, I'll start from the very beginning. It all started when I had a meeting a few days ago with the equity firm wanting to invest in my restaurants. This was the major deal I was telling you about, you know, a life-changer. I had a few drinks with them after the presentation. Not too many, but enough to be a little buzzed." *More than a little buzzed, but I cannot tell him this.* Dan nodded his head as Paul continued his story. He went through the blinding light, him passing out, and then waking up with a split lip and swollen eye.

"When the blinding light shone in my eyes, I swerved and hit a tree," Paul continued, "and I checked the damage on the right front fender of the car, but it was so dark. The next thing I knew I was waking up on the ground with a pounding headache. I was puzzled but somehow managed to get in my car and begin to drive home. I did remember there was a detour sign there, one confusing me. I could not remember the sign being there before on that day. When I drove back there again, the sign was gone. I know you think I'm nuts, but that's not even the worst half of it. I got home and staggered up to bed. I must have been drinking more than I thought, as I had a terrible hangover. But, the fact was, I didn't drink too much. It was like in the movies when someone is drugged and can't remember."

"Did you really get caught up in the moment and drink more hard liquor than you thought? It can happen to people. Hard liquor can sneak up on you," Dan said, still rubbing his chin with his hand and thinking.

"I didn't think so, but the worst was to come. The next morning I got up, went outside, and looked at the car again before Trisha got up. I just wanted to see the damage in the light. All I could see were the dents in the fender, so I knew I had hit something. Then I walked around the back of the car, and the trunk seemed to be open. I opened it and... and, well, there was a bloody, dead body in my car. With all that blood there, I vomited and was so sick."

For a moment, Dan looked shocked and couldn't begin to comprehend what Paul was saying. "Look, I think you should have called the police then. They could have found out what had happened," Dan said, eyeing his son carefully.

"But Dad, the worst part was Trisha came out and I told her I would be right in. I went in and well, we had sex. I did not have the nerve to tell her our dreams were about to be crushed. I went back outside, and I checked the trunk one more time. You are not going to believe me, but the body... it was gone! It looked like a body had never been there. I started to question even having a hallucination."

"Look, son, are you okay, are you taking drugs? This story, so far, is unbelievable. I mean, these kinds of circumstances just don't happen. I'm really concerned about you."

"Here, look at this. When I took my car to get it fixed at the body shop, Matt called and said this was on my windshield."

Dan took the note and read it. Cut out letters from a magazine on plain paper. **I know what you did and I think you are missing something**. Dan stared at the note and then back at Paul. Paul had always been truthful with him, but he was finding it hard to believe his son was innocent, and maybe his son had hit someone and gotten rid of the body. He shook the thought from his head, but still... Paul's story was difficult to swallow.

"Okay, first of all, I believe you," Dan said, almost stepping out on a limb because he thought he knew his son. "I'll back you on this, but first we have to decide how I can help you. I do have a friend, named Andy Marx, who has retired from the police force in Milwaukee and has moved here. He is a private investigator now. We went to high school together and played sports together, even were in the military together. I stayed in and he got out and became a cop. He's a good man and maybe we can get him to help us out. I would not tell Trisha anything about this yet. We will handle this through Andy and see what he can do. There may be a point when police must come in and handle the rest. I just want you to realize this. Be honest and tell the truth. It's the best we can do. I'll call him right now."

Chapter 9

Andy Marx answered the phone. He had been thumbing through the missing kid and grandpa file when Katy put the call through from his old friend, Dan Taylor.

"Hey, Dan, how are you? It's good to hear from you."

"Well, good to hear from you, too, but not under these circumstances," Dan said.

"Oh, no, what's happened?"

"Well, I wanted to know if my son, Paul, could come over to your office to see you. I am afraid something is wrong, but we need some advice because we really don't know where to start. It's something I don't want to talk about on the phone."

"I was just about to leave the office for a little while, but I can hang around until you get here."

"Thanks, Andy. It should take us about twenty minutes," Dan said. "See you in a few."

Andy hung up the phone. He waved goodbye to Mike and Katy as they made their way out the door to head home. He leaned back in his chair and turned to face the picture of him receiving his commendation for the work he had done in the Allison Branch case. He held the picture in his hand and thought of the events he had dealt with in his police career.

Andy heard a knock on the door, startling him from his recall of the day he was shot by Allison Branch. He rubbed his aching shoulder near the wound and saw Dan Taylor and his son at the door. He unlocked the door and let them in.

"Hi, Dan, it's so good to see you. My partners have left for the evening. Why don't you both come back to my office?" Andy said. "And you must be Paul. Your dad has told me so much about you."

They shook hands and Paul said, "Nice to meet you, Mr. Marx."

"Please call me Andy," Marx said, smiling at Paul. "Please sit down."

Dan opened the conversation. "Look, Andy, Paul may be in some kind of trouble. I'm not sure what kind of trouble because the events and story he's about to tell you seem too bizarre to be real. Go ahead, son. Tell him what you know."

"Well, Mr. Marx..."

"It's Andy, please."

"Okay, Andy."

Paul retold the story and Andy listened. Paul mentioned the meeting and leaving after drinking. He recounted the blinding light, his cut lip, and black eye, which was still visible. He told Andy how he saw the bloody body. Paul went on and described the body being gone and how he had planned to clean out his trunk, fearing he was being framed. Then he showed Andy the note left on his windshield.

Andy studied the note and remembered the ones Mike had gotten from Allison. This could be tied to someone who had it out for him, just as Allison had it out for Mike. He thought more and then looked up from the note. "Okay, look, this is something for the police to look at, Dan. I'm sure they would better handle this. Just go in and tell the truth, give them the facts and then let the case be investigated."

"No, wait," Dan blurted out. "I was hoping you would be the one to investigate. I trust you, and some folks around here I do not. I fear since Paul and his businesses are doing so well there will be a rush to judgement, and there are people who would love to see Paul go down in flames."

"I understand, but you do understand, Dan, I have two partners in this business and putting my neck out there also involves them putting their necks out there, too. I am going to have to share it with them. Talking my partner into this is tough because he is a prosecuting attorney. We both have reputations and can't be sidestepping justice."

"I realize this," Dan said to Andy, pointing to the note. "It is obvious someone is trying to frame my son and take him down. They want something from him, whether it is money or just to see him crash. There's something fishy here, and I think you would agree."

"Could you both step out for just a second and let me call my partner?" Andy asked. "You can wait in the outer office."

Andy dialed Mike and told him the story. Mike was hesitant at first.

"Andy, you know the old saying, 'No good deed goes unpunished', right?"

"I do, but there's something about this makes me think it's a setup. There is no body, no motive, and no weapon. I'd like to do this for Dan and his son. I'm as fearful as you are, but maybe if I can narrow some things down, we can get a few good leads and then send it to the cops. It would be like old times, two guys going after the bad guys."

Mike was quiet and thinking about the risk involved. They had escaped all the craziness, and now, they were possibly getting back into the world of chasing crazy people again. The thought of this made him shift to Katy's feelings. He was married now and had responsibility, something he had avoided before. He wanted to keep her safe and doing safe things in their life was now a priority, especially since they wanted to start a family. Saying yes to this one without her knowing would be hard.

"Look, Andy, I'm okay with it, but I have to explain to Katy the kind of case we're talking about here and what it may involve. It is something I must do before I say yes. Let me call you in an hour. This is not something to take lightly. You know how Katy worries."

"Thirty minutes," Andy said. "I don't want to have them leave without an answer."

"All right, thirty minutes." Mike said, hanging up. He looked up, saw Katy fixing dinner, and wondered how she would take this news. This case was more out of the ordinary, and there was no way to know how dangerous it would get. She wanted a baby and, if it did happen, he didn't think she's going to want the new father to be chasing dangerous criminals around again. Mike went to the kitchen and asked Katy to please sit with him at the table. He had to ask her a few questions.

When she was seated, she smiled at him and reached over to hold his hand. "What's on your mind?" she asked.

"Well, Andy just called from the office. He wants to take a case from a friend who went to high school with him. I listened to the case, and, well, it's not really the easiest."

"Now wait, Mr. Parsons, let's not beat around the

bush here. It is dangerous. I can tell because you would not be asking if it wasn't. You know how I feel about dangerous encounters with criminals. You know I am not cut out from the same cloth."

"Honey, listen, Andy can do the heavy investigating. I'm just the legal guy."

"I know Andy. He will talk you into it, saying you are a great psychologist, and you know people. I am sure you do, but I don't know. You understand how badly I'd love to be a mom."

"I do know, and we will keep working on it. But you know I'll be careful not to involve myself in the chase."

"No more half-truths, you promised me," Katy said, starting to get a tear in her eye.

"Okay, look, Marx saved my life, more than once. I owe him, and I think I can do this one for him. Please understand this. This is the truth. I want to help with this one."

Katy rubbed her forehead, and Mike could see the worry lines begin to form on her face. He reached across the table, stood from his chair, and walked to her. He gently placed his hand on her cheek. He bent down and kissed her on her forehead. "It will be okay, I promise."

"Okay, but you can't promise it will be okay, you just hope it will. Mike, I love you and want us to have a child. Please, please if you are going to say yes, you must be careful. I need you with me."

Mike leaned down and kissed her on the lips. "After dinner, I'm all yours," he said, his smile melting her like when he used to come in the bar at Nick's place. She could rarely say no to her man. She wanted to this time. But, she did not and now Mike and Andy Marx were a team again and this scared Katy O'Neal Parsons to death.

Andy had hung up after the second call back from Mike. He called Dan and Paul back into his office.

"Well, it looks like I'm going to work for you. Tomorrow, Mike, my partner, will have the contract and agreements drawn up. You can pay my retainer then."

"Andy, I really appreciate this more than you can possibly know. I owe you one," Dan Taylor said.

"Okay, we'll start tomorrow," Andy said. "I'd like to keep the note and look at it more. Any other evidence you come across in the meantime, you get in touch with me. There are rules to follow so none of us gets in trouble with the law. My partner is good with law, and he can keep us all on the right side of it. Remember, you include us in everything. You cannot go out there rogue and step in shit without us knowing. You call me when you have a thought or idea, don't be investigating. You leave it to us. You start going rogue, we are done, and I turn it over to the cops. Paul, I will need a list of friends and business acquaintances. Phone numbers and addresses would be important."

"You got it," Dan said, shaking Andy's hand. Dan and Paul left the office after exchanging information and phone numbers. The old chase Andy had missed was now on again. He felt some exhilaration and some fear about saying yes to keep this a private investigation. One thing about Andy Marx, if he had a fault, it was his loyalty to others and his willingness to come to their rescue. Andy Marx had always had "hero juice." Now, back on the trail of a killer, it was Mike and Marx, partners again. He needed to help his friend. Rubbing his shoulder with its bullet scar, he knew he also needed to be careful.

CHAPTER 10

Paul Taylor had finally gone home to Trisha. He was mentally exhausted and the meeting with the investors was coming up soon. He needed rest but the work was so important to him right now. He wanted so badly to share the events of the past couple of days with Trisha. Things were going so well, and he had this deal almost in his back pocket. This just did not seem like the right time to fill her in on these events. Although since he had talked to his dad, he felt like she needed to know.

She threw her arms around him and kissed him as he came through the front door. She was happy to see him, and she knew when he failed to hug her back, there was something wrong. He walked her over to the couch and sat her down. He sat next to her and began to tell her what he had been through.

"The other night, when I came home after the presentation, I had an accident. I mean, you know, I hit something. I really felt I was sober enough to drive. I came up on a detour sign I had not seen before, so I turned around and was following the detour on a road in the country. Suddenly, there was a blinding light, like a flash. Then I was out. I woke up on the ground with a pounding headache."

"Hold on, Paul, wait, this is not making sense."

"I know, Trish. It did not make sense to me either. I must have blacked out or the collision with a tree knocked me out. I had a cut lip and a black eye, you remember, seeing the black eye, don't you?"

"Oh, yes, Paul, I do. I just didn't think it was a big deal at the time. I don't remember seeing any dents on your car. I mean it's not a big deal we can always get the car fixed," she said, putting her hand to the side of his face.

"Yes, but there is more, much more. I went around to the back of the car and the trunk seemed to be popped open. I lifted the trunk, and I swear I saw a bloody dead body in the back of my trunk!"

"Paul, you can't be serious! Surely, you must have drunk too much. You came inside and we made love. You remember, don't you?" she asked, with a pouty look.

"Yes, I remember, Trish, of course, I do. I just need to tell you, when I went back out to look in the truck again there was no body. It was like it was never there, like I imagined it."

Paul looked around, as if he knew Trisha thought he was crazy. He had to find another way to tell this story. This surely was not going to make sense to Trisha. He didn't know what to do or say next. All he knew was that he needed to tell her he might be in trouble. He needed to tell her about the note.

"Look, Trisha, I went to Matt's Body Shop to take the car and get it fixed. I left the car there. Matt called me to say he had found a note on the windshield someone had left. I have a copy of the note," he said, handing it to her.

Trish's face turned into a look of deep concern. She looked up with a surprised look on her face and back down to the note again and read it again.

I know what you did and I think you are missing something

"What could it possibly mean?" She asked, wincing with every word as she read it aloud this time. "This really scares me, Paul, I mean, what have you done? You are not capable of doing something this evil. I know you, and you are such a good man. What are you going to do?"

"Well, I went to Dad's and talked to him. We went to meet with a friend of his, Andy Marx, a private investigator, in Springfield. They are going to look into it. He was torn between taking the case or just turning it over to the cops. He told dad he would take the case," Paul said, looking around the house, knowing if this went public, he could lose all of this, he could lose everything he had worked so hard to build. He might even lose Trisha. He hung his head.

The Silver Lake Equity Firm investment offer was an iffy deal but was what he was shooting for all along. He was so damn close; he could smell it and now this. He looked at Trisha and, in his own mind; he wondered if they would both survive this and what was this all about, he was not quite sure. As the days went by, he felt less safe and was wondering when the next note or knock-out punch would come.

Andy looked through the list of names Paul had left earlier that morning. He studied the list looking through the names and where they worked and lived.

He was interested in the connections Paul had, how long he had known each one, and if they were friends or business acquaintances. Andy would mull this list over for quite some time. He shuffled the papers looking through friends first, then business acquaintances, and then family. He was sure in most cases he had, many times the victims knew who their assailants were.

Andy continued to shuffle through the papers. Mike walked in and sat across from Andy at Andy's desk. Andy looked up and started the conversation.

"I've been looking through this list," Andy said. "I've been wondering, maybe if you want to look at half this list and categorize some of these people, maybe help me out with some profiling."

"Now wait just a second, my friend. I talked to Katy last night, and she's not so sure she wants me to get involved in any of these cases. I think she would rather have me do the legal work. She really wants to have a child."

"OK, but look, you know you are a good psychological profiler. I need you on these cases. You can talk her into it, can't you?"

"Man, I don't know, Andy. I mean, I think she's willing to let me do something about this after I talked to her, but I don't think there's any way I should be doing this. I put her through a lot in the past." Mike wanted to say no. But deep down, the idea of working with Andy again had intrigued him, and he felt there was no way he was going to fight this.

"Well?" Andy questioned.

"Okay, okay, I guess you got me. Working with you once again has certainly intrigued me. I don't know how I'm going to tell her this, but I'm going to say yes."

His answer brought a big smile to Andy's face, and he pushed the papers over to Mike. They began to shuffle through the names and classify the peoples' names, addresses, and phone numbers. They were working together again.

Partners again, M & M Private Investigators! The sound of it rang in Mike's ears. He had always wanted to do this. The attorney thing was his profession. Profiling and solving crimes were his passions. The case was just beginning, and like so many times before, Mike had no idea what they were getting into.

Chapter 11

Paul left for work the next day thinking what might have happened. He was trying to put together his thoughts about the light, his cut lip, his black eye. He was trying to understand just what had taken place. He knew he saw the body in the back of the trunk. He also knew the body was gone.

He asked himself if he thought he should turn himself in to the police. He was unsure, scared, and worried. He had worked so hard to get to this point in his life and job. Today he had one more preparation before he met for the final time with the equity firm.

He had begun to prepare extensive notes for the final preparations that he would discuss with his partners today. He had wanted this for Trisha and himself for so long. She had been by his side from the very beginning of this journey. Through thick and thin, he had risen from working odd jobs, to creating a business on the verge of being successful beyond his wildest dreams. Paul was the first to arrive at the restaurant and decided, for now; he had to shake the mysterious thoughts from his mind. Today had to be all about the presentation, and he needed to be at his best.

—▲—

Mike and Andy had arrived at the office earlier than Katy had. They were in the meeting room, shuffling through some papers and notes in the file Dan Taylor had left for Andy. They went over the list of acquaintances and friends, people Dan and Paul both knew. Most of the names were not eye-catching, but there were a couple catching Andy's attention.

"There are a couple of names looking more interesting than some of the others, but before we do, let's make some categories. There may be some people on this list who are looking for some way to frame Paul. For instance, look at, say, friends from high school," Andy said.

"Yeah, good idea. What about business partners?" Mike asked.

"It would be my first choice," Andy replied.

They began to categorize the names into groups and then place them on sticky notes on a white board near the table of the meeting room. They placed the names of Dan and Paul in the middle of the board. A bit lower on the board, they put four categories under Dan's and Paul's names.

The categories they decided on for Paul were friends, family, girlfriends, and business partners. For Dan's categories, they decided on old military friends, local friends, and family. Andy was looking at these categories closely and was trying to decide which one was the most important.

In all his days serving as a detective, Marx knew, most times, victims knew their attackers. They were either family or friends, even business partners. There would be questions to be asked of Dan and Paul. Certain questions were personal and uncomfortable. However, they were necessary.

Andy jotted down a few more notes on his computer and then looked at Mike. "Okay, Mike, let's start placing names in categories. Some may belong in more than one category. Go ahead and put them in multiple categories if they apply."

Paul's final meeting with Silver Lake would be held at Silver Lake's law firm. He and his partners were about to make the move they had always held as their highest goal. They had planned and worked as hard as any partners could possibly work, and they had stuck together. There were concerns, there were arguments, but, as a group, they had never wavered from the end game. They were almost there. Paul's team included an accountant, a law firm representing Taylor's Brew House, and a business negotiator. The Silver Lake Management Firm had brought their own people to handle their part of the business negotiations.

They sat together in the room and Paul was feeling nervous as his paranoia was catching up to him. *What if they know? Does anyone know? What do my partners know? This is all wrong, the timing, the moment before us is THE moment that we all have been waiting for. Damn it, I have to talk to Trisha, maybe Dad, anyone, someone. I'm physically sweating... geez.*

Paul came back to the moment. The thought of Trisha was stabilizing his thinking. He had to do this for her; he needed to do this for her. Trisha had stood firm with him through all the risk and all the good times and bad. He knew at this moment he must snap out of those thoughts or else this mega deal could go down the drain. The thought of his part of a seventy-five-million-dollar deal going from twenty restaurants to two hundred across the nation, well, it was impossible to say no.

Paul gathered himself as he looked around at his three partners and could see their excitement. The leader of the equity group, Jim Smothers, started the conversation. No one had a drink on the table. This was a serious moment of negotiation, and everyone had to be at their best. The thought of this deal, and all the residuals, was the life changing money that Paul had dreamed about for the past few years. The percentage of residuals was the question. They had agreed on twenty percent.

"It looks like all the paperwork is in order," Smothers said. "I am asking our attorney and business negotiator to present our offer and then your side can present the terms of your acceptance and, hopefully, we can come to the final deal."

After the presentation, one of the attorneys from the law firm for Taylor's Brew House, Charles Walls spoke, "It appears most everything on the presentation looks good to us. I will present our terms of agreement and, if everyone is on the same page, we can finalize the deal and sign."

Paul's pulse began to quicken. He could see the police charging into the room, arrest him for murder. The body had been found, and he was the main suspect. *Oh no, not now, this is the big one, please. Andy Marx and his team had to find out what was happening before it was too late. This deal had to go through and stay on the books.*

Charles finished his presentation, and all those present agreed upon the paperwork presented. All they had to do was sign. At that moment, Paul's phone rang. He saw it was his dad. He quickly excused himself while others around the table shook hands cementing the agreement before signing. His heartbeat faster as he thought; here it comes, the moment I have been paranoid about since the day it happened.

"Dad, hi. I'm in a meeting. Do you think I can call you back?"

"Paul, wait, listen to me. There is another note. This one was found on my door as I came home from the store."

"Oh, hell, what does it say?"

IF YOU WANT TO KNOW WHERE THE BODY IS YOU BETTER PLAY IT SMART. YOUR PRINTS ARE ALL OVER THAT BODY. TO START WITH, I'LL NEED TEN GRAND TO KEEP MY MOUTH SHUT. LEAVE THE MONEY AT THE PARK BY 10. TAPE IT UNDER THE MERRY-GO-ROUND. BETTER BE BY YOURSELF

Chapter 12

Mike and Andy put the finishing touches on their preparation for the investigation. The people they were most interested in were business associates; although family did figure into the story, too. They certainly did, but right now two or three names stuck out in Andy's mind and Mike agreed.

First there was a long-term connection with an associate that Paul had met in college, Dennis Tolton. They had instantly become friends when they got on campus. They seemed to have the same goals in the restaurant business and in life. They often hung out together, Dennis and his girlfriend, Lydia, and Paul and his girlfriend, Trisha. When Paul and the other partners expanded, Dennis left the company and took his share with him.

"Dennis never made it as big as Paul and the others and maybe he regretted the move," Mike said, rubbing the new goatee he was sporting. "Maybe he is the one that is trying to set him up. I am wondering why he wasn't included in the expansion. Paul never explained it in the descriptions he gave of these folks."

Andy stood up and walked back over to the board with the sticky notes on it. "Somehow, it doesn't fit to me. The guy had a nice share when he left the company, a cool two million, in fact. He had his money and doesn't look like he would have a motive."

"Maybe, but I still think he seems to be a person of interest," Mike said.

"True. What about this Lee Hamlin?" Andy asked, while flipping through the notes Paul had provided to them. "Says here he was a friend from high school and is in the same business, just a different company. Maybe he's jealous of Paul's success. It's possible."

"Yeah, Paul noted here Lee had small success but wasn't quite on par with what Paul's company is accomplishing. Maybe he's got the green envy bug," Mike said, as he rose from his chair. "I have to get home. I've had enough for one day."

Andy looked up briefly, "Go ahead, partner. I'm going to make some plans on which we need to investigate and what other people we need to see. I have one more person of interest here, Mike. What about Paul? Do you think he could have done this?"

Mike put on his jacket and walked back in front of Andy's desk. "I didn't want to say so because you and his dad are friends, but I believe I was pointing at him all along. He may have been drunk and hit the body. He could have put the body in the trunk, possibly even disposed of the body."

"It could be a wild goose chase," Andy said, raising his eyebrows in concern. "I can't really think he would do something like that. I know Dan pretty well, and I never took him for one who would let his son get away with that kind of irresponsibility."

"Don't rule it out; as you have told me many times

before, everyone is a suspect until you rule them out. Look, I have to go, I'll see you tomorrow."

Mike waved and walked out the office door. Andy heard the door shut and went to lock it. He came back, sat down at his desk, and tapped his pen lightly on his desk, questioning himself as to why he wanted to rule Paul out as a suspect so quickly. Mike was using his own rule against him. Andy knew better and decided that he was calling it a day, too. He grabbed his coat, headed out the door, locked it behind him and went to his car.

He started the car and sat there for a few moments thinking. *I know better, and Mike was right. I couldn't rule Paul out, not yet anyway. He would have to be investigated like every suspect.*

It was 9:00 pm and Paul was waiting in his car at the park. He was told to go there and tape the money under the merry go round. He knew he was taking a risk by paying this money, because it may not be the only time. He was nervous as he sat there with the $10,000 on the front seat. He looked around for another car, another person, or anyone else that was there in the park. He saw no one in the area.

Paul nervously walked out of his car towards the merry go round. The dew on the grass made his tennis shoes wet. He quickly grabbed the roll of tape from his jacket and put the money under the merry go round. He looked all around one more time. He saw no one, and then made his way back to the car.

Paul waited in his car for a few more minutes, and he saw no one go after the money. He figured that he couldn't wait any longer. He knew Trish would be calling for him if he didn't come home soon. He started the car and drove away from the park. He now wondered if he had done the right or wrong thing. He thought he might know soon enough.

Paul pulled into his garage, parked the car, and then looked all around the outside. He constantly felt he was being followed. He never could see anyone and that started him thinking that maybe he really did hit someone, killed them, and dumped the body himself. *Was my drinking that bad? Holy shit, I couldn't have done that, could I?*

He shook the thought and headed to the living room where he found Trisha watching television. He put his keys on the table and walked over to her. He bent down and kissed her, and her fragrance was something he had not remembered her wearing before.

"New perfume?" he asked, siding up closer to her and putting his arm around her. "Smells great."

"Something I picked up today, just for you. It's a new one I got from the boutique over on National Street. It's called 'Secret Temptation'. I was hoping you would like it."

"It's intoxicating."

Trisha got up from the couch and pulled Paul to his feet with both hands. She led him to the bedroom and shut the door. She took off her top, revealing her ample breasts and protruding nipples. She was aroused, and Paul felt the same.

"You do like what you see, don't you?" she asked, moving in closer and starting to unbutton his shirt.

"Hell, yes. You're stunning and so, so sexy," he said, running his hands through her blonde hair as he totally forgot about the merry-go-round at the park. Paul took off his shirt and Trisha removed his pants. They stood totally naked before each other.

Paul started to pull Trisha towards the bed, but she quickly grabbed his shoulders and turned him so she could sit him down in the chair. She climbed up on top of him and started kissing his neck. She was passionate, strong, and took Paul inside her. She began to thrust lustfully, almost hard, and Paul was enjoying this. He began to thrust back inside of her as the pace between them began to pick up. They were in a rhythm now, and she began to moan and call his name. They both exploded passionately as Trisha fell limp against Paul, feeling the aftershocks of their glorious moment and totally out of breath.

"Wow, that was amazing," Paul said, between breaths. "I don't know what has gotten into you, but I sure like it."

"Just trying to help relieve the stress I know you're feeling. It never hurts to try something new, right?"

"I love you, Trish. I promise that this will be over soon. The friends of my dad will get this investigation going, and we'll get to the bottom of this."

They showered and got under the covers together. Trisha laid her head on Paul's chest and asked, "Do you promise this will all be over soon?"

"Yes, I think so. We have to believe the investigators will come up with a solution soon. My dad said they are very good."

"Well, I hope so. We can't have this thing over our heads forever. You've worked so hard for what we have. I'm so proud of you."

Paul looked at the ceiling while he stroked her hair. "Thanks, dear. Life will be just what we dreamed about, you'll see."

Trisha fell asleep on Paul's chest as he lay wide awake, thinking about what would happen to him if he really had a blackout and did all this. All his dreams and all that hard work down the drain. He would be in prison and Trisha, well... he just couldn't think about that.

MALCOLM TANNER

CHAPTER 13

Lee had a good hiding place for the money. He needed to stash it away because he had a meeting to go to at the Chamber of Commerce. There at the meeting, he could have his own mental fun looking Paul in the eye and knowing that his plan was working. Paul had no idea who was after his money. Lee entered the old farmhouse and stashed the money up in the attic. He then got down from the ladder, took it around back and leaned it up against the house. He then got the key from under one of the floorboards and unlocked the freezer. He wanted to make sure that the body was still there.

As he unlocked the freezer and lifted the lid, he saw the frozen stiff body there, untouched, and in the same position. He slowly closed the lid knowing that he still was in control of the situation, as long as the body was there. Lee was lucky in this game, so far, and he didn't intend on stopping.

It was noon and the Chamber meeting was about to begin. Paul had walked in with his partner, Ted Jansen, and they sat down at the table closest to the door. Other members were mingling with soft drinks or water as the program had yet to start.

"Damn, Paul, we're almost home. The deal is being finalized and we sit here among the Chamber elites, just about to become one of them," Ted said, taking a sip of his water. "I'm excited, aren't you?"

"Yeah, I'm excited, too," Paul said, not sounding as if he were. "Hey, isn't that Lee Hamlin over there? He's talking to that hot girl from the local television station."

"Yeah, that's him. He told me once in high school that you stole all his girlfriends. Man, he was dorky back then!" Ted exclaimed.

"I felt rather sorry for him back in those days. He came from a pretty rough home. His parents never let anyone come over. I think he was embarrassed about it, and I think they might have had something to hide. I'm going to go over and talk to him."

"You just want to steal the hot TV girl from him, don't you?" Ted asked, trying to get a reaction from Paul.

"Oh, come on, man. You know better than that," Paul said, looking back over his shoulder at Ted. "I got a hot one at home."

Paul walked on over to Lee and his new acquaintance. He waited quietly and did not interrupt the conversation. When it was over, Lee shook hands with the girl, and she turned to walk toward another guest she knew.

"Hello, Lee," Paul said, reaching out his hand to shake Lee's. "It's good to see you. Nice looking girl you were talking to."

"Yeah, she's the new anchor from the station. She was just asking a few questions about people in the room, and, yes, she is very nice looking. I see you picked up on that like you did with my girlfriends in high school."

"C'mon, Lee, I never took any of your girls," Paul said, with a smile. "Well, anyway, how is your business doing?"

"It's starting to come around. Hit a rough spot a couple of months ago when I couldn't keep employees. It's getting better. And you? I hear you have hit the big one. I always knew you were going to be that guy," Lee said, knowing in his mind he wanted to reach out and choke Paul.

"How did you know that?" Paul asked him. "We haven't put that out for public knowledge yet," Paul said, wondering who leaked that information or how that got to someone like Lee Hamlin. Strange.

"Rumors, just rumors. You know how people talk in a small town."

"Well, keep it under your hat, Lee. We have some things to tie up first before it's official."

"Will do. Hey, good luck and hope everything works out well. I need to get back to my table."

"Hey, Lee, good luck, man. I hope you get everything you want."

They shook hands and walked away from each other. As he walked, Lee's mind was racing. *Yeah, you have everything I want. I already have ten thousand big ones from you, and I hope to get more. No, Paul, I really don't think you want me to be successful. You like holding me down, just like my father, my mother, and most everyone else in my life did. I really do hate you, Paul Taylor, and I will get what I want. I'm just getting started!*

After the meeting, Paul and Ted walked to his car.

Paul noticed another note on his windshield. He hurried to the car and took it and folded it quickly, stuffing it in his pocket.

"What was that?" Ted asked, as Paul unlocked the vehicle.

"Just a playful note from Trisha. She must have come by while we were at the meeting. Come on, get in, and I'll take you back to the office. I need to go check one of our locations. They said they are short of help."

"Sure, Paul. Sounds good. I'm going to call the lawyers and see how the paperwork is going with some of the investors. Damn, when I think of it, I can't believe where we are right now," Ted said, buckling his seat belt.

"Yep, my friend, we're in a pretty good place," Paul said. But after seeing the note, he really didn't believe they were. He had to go see Mike and Andy. He drove on, dropping Ted off at the office. Ted got out, waved goodbye, and went inside.

Paul pulled out the note and read it. This was the third one and he was torn on what to do. Someone was asking for money again. Someone was trying to ruin him. Someone seemed to have control of him.

DON'T KEEP GOING TO THOSE PRIVATE EYES. THAT WILL BE A BIG MISTAKE! I'VE BEEN WATCHING. NO MORE OPEN PLACES. TWENTY THOUSAND AND LEAVE IT UNDER THE DUMPSTER IN A BAG, WRAPPED AND TAPED, AT 1:00 AM BEHIND THE CAR WASH. NO INVESTIGATORS!

Paul read it one more time. His mind was swimming. He had reached the pinnacle of his career. His hard work and effort were about to be all for naught if this person called the cops. He had to end this somehow, some way.

This is all coming down so fast. Two weeks had gone by, and no body, no suspect, no weapon. It sure is looking like me. What did I do? Did I black out on my feet? Did I kill someone? Someone knows, and we have to find that person. This could be the fucking end of me. Do I take this to Marx and let them try to catch the person, or do I take the money and keep my mouth shut? What does this guy have on me? I can't lose Trisha, our house, the business. No way. It is a nightmare. Someone took that body out of my trunk. It was not my imagination.

Paul was furious and could only imagine wearing prison orange. He put the car in drive and headed to M & M Private Investigators. He was done with being threatened. They had to catch whoever was doing this. Paul wanted to believe in himself and that was his bottom line. It was the answer to all his questions in life. He trusted himself to do right. He always had. But for the very first time, doing right, at this very moment, was his biggest struggle of his life.

CHAPTER 14

Katy was lighter than air. She was just getting to the office. It was 1:00 and she knew Mike would be there because he had taken his lunch today. She walked in the door and made her way to Mike's office. He was gone, so she put something she had in her hands on the desk and went to Andy's office. She knocked on the door, and Andy hollered "Come in!"

"Hi, guys. Looks like you are hard at it. Do you think I can borrow Mr. Parsons for just a second, Andy?" she asked.

"Sure, sure thing, Katy. Just don't let him off the hook too long, we might be getting closer to narrowing down our list of people," Marx said, hardly taking his eyes off the papers on his desk.

Katy and Mike both walked out together headed down the hall to Mike's office. When he stepped inside, he saw two balloons on his desk. One pink and one blue. He turned quickly to her and asked, "Does this mean what I think it means?"

"Yes, I really am pregnant!" Katy exclaimed, unable to hide her unbridled happiness. She threw her arms around Mike, and he pulled her close to him. She began to cry real tears of joy that ran down her beautiful cheeks and onto Mike's shirt. He held her shoulders and looked into her moist eyes, hugging her once more.

"I'm so excited. You're going to be the best mom ever. I don't know what to say, but we'll be the best parents ever!"

"Oh, Mike, I'm so happy, words can't describe what I'm feeling. I love you so much."

Mike opened his door and yelled down the hall, "Hey, Marx, get in here, quick."

Andy hurried down the hall and entered the office. He saw the balloons.

"Yep, that's right, my friend. We're going to be parents," Mike said.

"Really? No kidding, Geez, you two, that's great! Well... congratulations. This is great news!"

They all shook hands and hugged. Andy went to get his best bottle of Woodford. He came back in and poured a glass for Mike and himself. Knowing Katy was pregnant, he grabbed a soft drink out of the cooler for her.

"A toast. To my best friends. May you be the best parents of one happy and healthy child."

They clinked glasses and started to have a cheery conversation when they heard the front door open. "I'll be right back, you two," Andy said. "I'll see who came in." Andy continued down the hall shaking his head and smiling at the good news. He got to the front of the office and there stood Paul Taylor with another note in his hand.

"Hello, Paul. More trouble?" Andy asked.

"Yes, I think more than I can handle, Andy."

"Look, I'll get Mike and you can go into my office.

We were just celebrating the fact that Katy is pregnant."

"Sorry to interrupt," Paul said, looking down and wondering if he would ever have the chance to be called "dad". It was beginning to look bleak.

Andy went back and asked Katy if he could borrow Mike back for a second and that Paul Taylor was out front. Mike left the office, turned and smiled at Katy. "I love you," were the words he mouthed to her and blew her a kiss. Katy didn't want Mike to go as she was having the best moment of her life. She also knew that if Paul Taylor had come back, something more sinister must be taking place. This was something that she had on her mind lately, and it was her newest test to her new-found strength. She began to doubt if she could be strong, but she quickly shook it off and sat down in Mike's office chair. Her mind began to drift.

Paul came into the office, and they sat around the conference table. Paul was having a hard time looking either Andy or Mike in the eye. With his head down, he began to let him know his troubles.

"I'm afraid I've messed up. I had a note and was told to leave $10,000 at the park. I know I shouldn't have done that, but I was scared. I didn't want Trisha and me to lose everything we worked for," Paul said as he looked up from his gaze at the floor. He saw Andy's face begin to redden. "Now I've got a second note."

"Damn it, Paul. We should call the cops right now. I told you that you should bring everything to us, and I mean EVERYTHING!" he shouted explosively, making Paul return his gaze to the floor. "I told you that we were out if this happened. My partner and his wife are expecting a child. He doesn't need this shit right now either."

"I know... I'm sorry... I... just didn't think," Paul replied, feeling his world crashing in.

"Look, I served with your dad and there's nothing stronger than the military bond. We'll give you one more chance but you need to walk the straight and narrow. I'm not going to put these good people at risk. If you pull another stunt like this, we are done, and we will be the ones calling the police."

"I understand, and I promise I won't do that again. Someone is out there trying to frame me. This needs to end. I'll do anything you ask me to do, but please find this guy," Paul said.

"Let me see the note," Andy said, holding his hand out. Andy read it and passed it over to Mike.

"This time $20,000?" Mike asked, looking at them both. "That is pretty bold, wouldn't you say?"

"Yeah, that is brazen, almost too brazen," Andy said, feeling that maybe he was wrong about Paul's innocence.

"Look, Paul, you go home and explain to your fiancée what kind of trouble you're in. We'll make a plan to try and catch this guy. Be at your office by ten tomorrow, and we'll have a plan ready to catch this guy."

Paul shook hands with both and left the office of M & M Investigators. Andy and Mike continued the conversation.

"You still think he's innocent?" Mike asked. "This episode seems so contrived, and I'm finding it harder to believe this guy."

"Like I said, Mike, I have to help Dan. It's my loyalty to the guy. I know he would do the same for me. I know I'm taking a big chance here. Just give it one more try. I still believe Paul, although I know it is getting tougher to do."

"All right, but if this kind of thing happens again, I am for sure out. I owe you a lot and I will hang with you for a bit longer. Paul Taylor is making me more suspicious by the minute," Mike countered.

"All right, let's make the plan," Andy said, as he pulled out his legal pad and began to make notes.

It was 9:00 PM that night and Paul had to sit down with Trisha and let her know that someone was trying to blackmail him.

"Look, someone is out there that hates me, and I aim to find out who it is. You know that I've got my dad's friend, Andy, and his partner, Mike, helping me. I have to go out shortly and place the money near the tennis courts in town."

"Honey, this sounds really dangerous. Are you sure you should be doing this? Why don't you just go to the police?"

"There is too much at stake, and, well, you know my trouble with the cops. Ever since that incident at the restaurant, they have been on my case."

"Paul, we have a good life here. Things have been going so well. Are you sure that you want to take the risk doing this and end up in all kinds of trouble? You know I love you so much and that soon we can be married. Are we risking us?" she asked, looking at him with her captivating eyes.

"Trisha, I don't want to hurt our chances at the life we have dreamed of. This has to be solved," he said, nervously tapping a pen on the table. "I can't go on much longer until I find out who is doing this. I'll be leaving in about ten minutes, and I am hoping their plan works. They want to identify a vehicle or person that is picking this money up."

"Please, be careful. You mean everything to me. Just watch out for yourself and come back to me safe."

Trisha stood up and moved behind Paul and began

to rub his neck and shoulders. The muscles in his neck and shoulder area were taut, like a bow string pulled back and ready to release its arrow. Her hands kneaded his tension until Paul was almost relaxed.

I just want this to be over. Everything was so perfect and yet, at this point, nothing seems perfect except the warm hands massaging me. She is an angel, my angel, and I am not going to give her up over this monster who is trying to intimidate me. The franchising deal is so perfect. It is our big dream and we have survived everything, and we will survive this episode.

Paul stood from his chair and faced Trisha. He kissed her lightly on the lips, and then she kissed back passionately, much harder and deeper than he had ever been kissed before. He began to breathe hard, and his passion began to grow. "We... I... can't right now. I need to meet them, and I can't be late," he said, wishing he did not have to go.

"Be safe, my love. I will be waiting for you," she said, rubbing his chest with her palms.

"I'll hurry home," Paul replied, feeling a fire for Trisha that was so new, even though they had been together for so long. *This guy has to be stopped. I can't lose this, especially this woman who has stood by me.*

They kissed once more, and Paul turned to leave. He went out the garage door, and Trisha heard the car start, the garage door open, and then she went to the front window to watch his car pull away. As soon as his car was out of sight, Trisha pulled out her phone and made a phone call.

CHAPTER 15

Mike and Andy left the office at 10:00 pm. They headed to the offices of Taylor's Brew House to meet Paul. They were talking along the way.

"Look, Mike, this could be very difficult and there could be some danger involved. Are you sure you want to go along?" Andy asked, as he drove south on Highway 13.

"Yes, I'm sure. When I told you I was in, I meant in all the way."

"You need to be careful, partner. This is starting to get on the dangerous side of things. You watch your back, my friend."

"I'll be careful; I can take care of myself."

They arrived at the office and saw Paul waiting for them in the parking lot. Andy surveyed all around the lot, looking for anything or anyone suspicious. He saw nothing and pulled in next to Paul's car. Paul got out, locked his car, and got in with Mike and Andy.

"Okay Paul, here's the plan..."

Andy explained to Paul what he needed to do. Paul understood and he returned to his car and was soon driving the ten-minute drive to Redfield Park. He arrived at the car wash near the park and got out with the package. Mike let Andy out on the other side of the park at a baseball field, where he could easily get close enough to get a few pictures or even confront whoever picked up the money. Mike drove the car back to the car wash to wait and watch. Andy texted Mike when he was settled. The plan was in place and they were ready.

Paul placed the fake money package and all the way back to the car wash he looked all around. He was hoping and praying that this situation would somehow come to an end. He had faith in Mike and Andy, mainly because his dad said nothing but good about his friend Andy Marx. Paul kept walking and saw nothing all the way to the car wash, where he walked around back and got into his car. Mike followed Paul back to Taylor's Brew House offices. When they arrived, they got out and went inside to Paul's office. Paul poured them both a glass of one of his best whiskeys.

"Look, Paul, I know we don't know each other very well. I've helped Andy, he's a great cop, and he will smoke this thing out. Don't worry."

"I know I screwed up, and you guys could think I'm just covering for myself. You have to believe me. Someone is out to get me and frame me for something I didn't do. I did see that body and there is a body missing, that is for sure," Paul said in rapid fire.

"Settle down, we do believe you," Mike said, not really sure if deep down inside that he did. "You leave this to us and don't give anyone any more money. You are going to have to trust us and, most of all, you can't hide things from us. We need to know everything."

Paul looked down and then back up to meet Mike's

eyes again. "It's just that Trisha and I have worked so hard to get where we are. I don't think I could handle it if something bad happens to us. I can't lose her. I am telling you everything. I haven't left anything out."

Mike could not help but think that this invisible person that was trying to blackmail Paul possibly did not exist. Mike promised Andy he would think of Paul as innocent until proved otherwise. But Paul seemed to be struggling and each time he had been with Paul or listened to him, he seemed more desperate. *Is he fooling us? He seems so intent that someone is doing this to him; I can't help but think he may be guilty. If we don't find a guy tonight, trying to pick up this fake money package, then I will not be sure about Paul Taylor. In all honesty, I'm really not too sure about him now.*

"Look, we do believe you. Andy is good, and if he finds someone out there, he's going to make sure they come to justice."

They both finished off their drinks quickly as Mike had a text from Andy, saying that he thought he saw something moving around the park, but he couldn't make out what it was. Marx took pictures, but he was afraid he wouldn't have anything. By the time Mike drove back, he would be ready to go. He told Mike to pick him up at the car wash.

"I have to go, Andy left me a text. He saw something but was not sure he could define it. I need to go pick him up."

"Well, thanks for helping me, Mike. You and Andy are great."

They shook hands and Mike left the office and got into this car. He started the engine and began to drive back to Redfield.

Mike began to drive away from the office and looked into the rearview mirror to see if he could catch any glimpse of movement. All he could see was Paul getting into his car and driving away. Wishing he could help Andy right now, Mike increased his speed... someone is out there possibly trying to frame Paul Taylor, or, maybe not.

CHAPTER 16

Mike waited for Andy to show up at the car wash. He had not heard from him since he left Paul's office. He was worried about this adventure. *Who was this guy framing Paul or was there even a guy? Andy's a good cop. That's what I told Paul. If anyone can solve this, it is Andy Marx. This Paul, he seems to be lost at this moment. Maybe he is the guy who really did it. Maybe he is making all kinds of excuses and wild stories to throw us off track. Maybe I should try to convince Andy that Paul is the one we need to look at as THE suspect. Andy is connected to his dad, and he may not like me saying it, but Andy has always trusted me to be honest with my feelings.*

Mike's thoughts were interrupted by a shadowy figure walking towards his car. It seemed to be coming at him, but Mike could see no face. In fact, the face was covered, and he could not make out who the person was. Mike gripped the handle of the pistol he kept in the console. He had gotten it out as soon as he left Paul's office. He was more careful these days, especially when he was in the car alone. He had promised Katy to stay away from all danger. He needed to be there for Katy.

Mike slumped lower in the seat hoping the dark figure would keep on walking and turn in a different direction. The figure was still coming directly at him. He took off the safety and was ready. The figure reached into the pocket of the hood he was wearing. Mike raised the gun and was ready to fire at the first notice of a gun appearing. The hand came out of the pocket with no gun, and the figure removed his facemask.

Lee had spies in several parts of Paul's life. Lee never showed up to pick up the package because he knew Paul was working with the investigators. He wasn't going to fall for their plots to catch him. He had done everything right, and he wasn't about to get caught doing anything careless. He had a bead on those guys, and they weren't going to be a step in front of him. He would be two steps ahead of them.

Lee wanted to go back to the farmhouse. He didn't want to relive his youth, but maybe by going there, he could bring back the reasons this plan was so important to him. He started to pick up speed as he turned onto the gravel road of the farmhouse. He felt just seeing the place would remind him of why he had to succeed. He could not fail because he couldn't take any more rejection. His speed was up to sixty on the gravel road as he looked down at the speedometer. As his anger rose, so did his speed.

The next curve was not kind to Lee. He went into a

dangerous skid, turning completely sideways. After correcting the wheel, he finally got control of the car. He slowed to a stop and put his head down on the steering wheel. He looked in the mirror and saw sweat rolling down his forehead, burning his eyes. *Damn Paul Taylor!* He drove away slowly heading back to town.

The hand came out of the pocket with no gun, and the figure removed his facemask. Mike's sweaty hand eased his grip on the gun, and he placed it back in the console. The figure was Andy.

Mike breathed a sigh of relief as he unlocked the door for Andy to climb in the front passenger seat. "You had me worried, partner," Mike said, as he started to breathe at a slower pace. "All I saw was this dark figure coming for my car and no face. I pulled the gun out. You should have called."

"Sorry, Mike. I was just upset that we are getting nowhere. This person, whoever it is, seems to lead a charmed life. Either they are smarter than us, or we have a suspect that seems to know our every move. They are one step ahead of us."

"Andy, look, I know you don't want to hear this, but maybe Paul is the one who is one step ahead of us."

"I don't know, Mike. You may be right. I sure don't want to think that way, but maybe we should be looking at him harder. Maybe we should even call the police."

"I'm not saying you have to do that. I'm saying that maybe we should consider what he says and what he does more carefully," Mike said, as he kept driving back down Campbell Street towards the office. "Have we investigated his past much? No, we haven't. Is it because you really don't believe he is the one or do you not want it to be Paul because Dan is your friend?"

"I admit that I have been trying to deny to myself that Paul could have committed this crime. I also admit that I really don't know Paul, and you could be right about him. But I could never imagine having to say to my friend that his son is the main suspect."

"Not saying you have to do that right now, but just don't throw it aside either," Mike said.

"I don't know... I really don't know."

They arrived back at the parking lot of their business. Mike let Andy out and said goodbye. He was headed home to Katy. Andy went to his car and got in heading for home, also. With his thoughts clouded with his friend, Dan, his son Paul, and knowing he had to go visit his dad tomorrow, Andy failed to notice a car was following him.

Chapter 17

Katy was glad to see Mike walk in the door. She had decided to wait up for him, watching television in the living room. When he came through the door, she immediately went to him, kissed him, and held him close.

"I was getting worried. I felt left out and abandoned when Paul came into the office, and Andy and you got busy with his problems while I wanted to celebrate our long-awaited news."

"I'm sorry about that, Katy," Mike said to her as he led her towards the couch so they could sit together. "I think Paul may have something to do with this missing body. Andy wants me to believe Paul. I'm just having trouble trusting him. It feels like he's leading us on this wild goose chase."

"You know people and have a good intuition about these things, Mike. You could be right. I haven't talked to him enough to really let you know what I think. But if you say that, it may be true."

"There's something wrong here. People don't just have bodies removed from the car at their homes. This seems so unlikely, that I can't get past thinking Paul could be a murderer."

"Have you even thought of the others on the suspect list?" Katy asked. "Does he sleep around on his girlfriend?"

"Interesting you ask that. Sometimes I think the same thing when it comes to spouses, girlfriends, boyfriends and the like. Jealousy is the main motivator in many crimes. You bring up something that also worries me about the case. I think we are barely scratching the surface."

"Well, let's forget about that for the moment and celebrate our new little addition to our family," Katy said, with the gorgeous smile that had made Mike fall in love with her.

"You're right. Enough for the day. Mrs. Parsons, I love you and I love us."

They turned off the lights and headed to bed.

Paul had gotten home and walked inside his home. His big, beautiful home was the one he and Trisha had planned for themselves. The next home would be bigger and even better. He didn't see Trisha right away and his phone buzzed. He answered it as he sat down at the kitchen table.

"Hello, Paul? It's Andy. I did a lot of surveillance and wanted you to know that we didn't come up with anything. I looked all over that park. I have nothing so far. Mike picked me up after letting you out and took us back to the office. I'm at home now."

"I hate to hear this, Andy."

"My theory is that someone writing these notes

knows you're talking to us. They have an upper hand and the note writer had to have known somehow that we are helping you. It signals to me that he may have people working with him. It's just my thoughts and nothing solid."

Paul froze and the hair on the back of his neck started to stand up. *Damn this is looking bad for me. Soon, they will be thinking it was me. They keep coming up with dead ends. Did I really do this and just can't remember?* "Thanks for that information, Andy. I guess we're back to square one," Paul said, as he fiddled with a pen that was on the table.

"Don't worry, Paul. We are still going to get to the bottom of this."

"Thanks, Andy. I'm sure you will. Talk to you later, and thanks again for trying to help me."

"You get some rest, Paul."

Paul put his head in his hands and then he looked at the wall directly across from him. He thought he was heading to jail. The cops would soon be informed, and he and Trisha would lose everything. He buried his head back into his hands. Two hands suddenly squeezed his neck muscles from behind, making Paul jump. He turned to see Trisha there.

"Damn, Trish, you startled me."

"Who was that on the phone?" she asked.

"It was Marx. They found nothing tonight. Soon, they will be pointing the finger back at me. It's just my luck that things would go this way. I'm convinced that they think I'm lying."

Paul, honey, this is not you. Give them time, they will find the answers," Trisha said, continuing to massage his aching neck, tight from all this high anxiety. "You know I believe in you and this will work out. Why don't you come to bed and see if I can relieve some of this tension you have developed?"

Andy had trouble sleeping so he got up and went to his home office desk. He began to sift through the suspect list again and make notes. In his mind, Andy thought they were done making theories and had to get to solid investigating and surveillance. The question was where to start. Andy wanted to know more about two or three people specifically.

One of those people was Lee Hamlin. He wanted to do some background on him and try to understand specific things about him. He wanted to know who his friends were, all about his past, and his parents. This Lee has perfect motivation. Then there were his partners.

You can't rule anyone out. There's Paul and his fiancée, Trisha. They could have done this together, and this story is a perfect cover for them. They both may have panicked. Is this dead body someone from Paul's past, someone that got in the way? We have to find the body, or there is no case. No dead body makes everything go away. They get away with it if we don't find a body. This will be difficult and delicate, but we have to make headway soon before this case goes completely cold...

Andy became more alert and began writing down names and searching his computer for anything that could give him a clue. He needed to interview some people and he would start with Paul and Trisha. Then he would do some surveillance on Lee Hamlin. Also, he would see if Lee would talk to him. He needed the information from each suspect's past. But he needed to follow some people, too.

The thing is Andy had no idea he was being followed, too. Someone needed some addresses on where those private investigators lived. Someone wanted to be able to know their every move. Andy was unaware of the presence of the vehicle parked near his place. The person in the vehicle was taking notes later while Andy was fast asleep.

CHAPTER 18

Throughout this whole scheme, Lee Hamlin had always had the upper hand. It was the day after the failed money drop, and he was heading towards a full boil. He knew Paul and his father were working with the private investigators. He saw them, he watched them, and Lee was ahead of the game. Of all the things Lee was, he wasn't dumb. In fact, Lee was so smart that the intricate scheme he had put together was now in jeopardy.

He stood in the middle of the living room floor of the old farmhouse, cursing them all under his breath. By this time, he had hoped to have $30,000 dollars with one more note to place for a bigger bonanza, one that could make his business get over the top and possibly ruin Paul's. But the investigators are getting in the way. This one last note would either make Paul cooperate, or he would leave the best note of all to the cops.

He stood there, unable to keep his hands from shaking. He had lived here, if you call it living. He was verbally abused and neglected by his parents. Grace Hamlin, his mother, just let it happen. She tried to keep Elmer from hitting Lee and his foster sister. She was too frail to stop him. Lee just remembered how horrible it was. He smelled the musty and dirty smells of the home. He heard the screams of his mother and the constant yelling of his father. His hands were shaking even more. He could hear him, stomping, cursing, and drunk as he could be. He could smell the whiskey breath of his father, as if he were standing right in front of him.

His childhood was a complete and utter failure by his parents to provide what Lee needed. He was his own man now, self-made and warped. His mind had given in to all that he had become. There was no one to guide him growing up in this world. He did it in his own twisted and demented way.

He had become the abuser after being abused early in his life. He often would sneak into his foster sister's room. He held his hand over her mouth as he would fondle her newly developed breasts. At sixteen, she was becoming womanly in her figure, and he wanted to have the carnal knowledge that other boys at school had discussed at the lunch table. No one had told him about sex. He did not know anything about the respect factor in sex. He was just trying to figure it out on his own.

She stopped his advances many times. She was afraid of Lee and finally left home at the very young age of sixteen, before Lee could do any more damage than he had already inflicted. She was away from Lee, and Lee had always resented her for leaving. When he found her again, working in Kansas City, he vowed to himself that she would someday come to him, and he would have her for his own. He remained in contact and finally found an avenue that would make her sit up and pay attention. That avenue was greed, and she wanted to play the game.

It was 6:00 am the next day and Andy was already at work. He had lined up a few appointments for Mike and him. He wanted to interview some people. Hopefully, he would get some kind of lead that would get the case moving. *A body, you need a body. Without a body, you have no case. Someone has to crack.* Just then Mike and Katy came in and waved to Andy as they passed the door to his office.

"Hey, partner, can you come in for a minute?" Andy took a sip of his black coffee.

"Sure thing," Mike waved to Katy as she moved along towards their office.

Mike sat down across from Andy, "What's up?"

"I'm feeling like we need to get out and interview some people. Some may agree to talk and some may not, but we have to see if we can get some information," Andy said, looking down at his list of suspects.

"I would agree, but where do you start?"

"I think we have to question Paul and Trisha. We have to find out if they really are innocent and that they had nothing to do with this missing body."

"Okay, I would agree, but if we have no body, do you expect them to crack?"

"Not sure, but we have to start there. It is the most logical place."

"What about Lee Hamlin? I think we should talk to him soon," Mike said, looking at Andy for some reaction.

"Interesting that you brought him up. I found some interesting stuff on the internet going back to where Lee attended school. I talked with someone from that community, and it seems he had a foster sister. I'd like to talk to her, too."

Mike took a deep breath, trying to put this all together. It was beginning to sound dark and evil to him. He wanted to not think of Paul and Trisha as murderers. Yet, he couldn't help but think he and Andy were grinding their gears against some immovable object and that immovable object was the dead body they could not find. Someone had to break. "Okay, who's first?"

"I want to talk to Paul and Trisha first. If they have some sort of resistance, then maybe there is something to follow. Lee would be next; he has a motive against Paul. Finally, we need to ask Lee about his foster sister and see how he reacts. After that, I want to talk to the partner who left the company. I'm going to call Paul and set up a time to talk to both of them. Mike, why don't you go to Lee's restaurant and try to find out where and when we can talk to him. Let's save the partners until tomorrow."

"All right, sounds good to me. Let me know, so I can work it into my schedule."

"Will do. I also have to finish up on that grandpa kidnapping case. I think I have a lead on that one. I'll follow up on something about that one today."

"Okay, give me a call when you have time. I'll be catching up on some legal stuff while you're doing that."

Andy finished up and headed out the door. He had a couple of leads to follow and a few phone calls to make. He would be busy.

He walked into the fall sunshine and saw that the clouds were beginning to partially block out the sun. He found it funny that he thought of it as deception by the clouds, trying to cover something up that was obvious. The sun is bright, clear, and makes the sky an even deeper blue. It was the sun that cleared things up and brought truth to the forefront. *I need to sift through these clouds of deception that were moving all around the truth, covering it, and hiding it from that deep blue sky that is the obvious answer. It had worked in all my investigations before. Where were the clouds coming from? Who was making them appear and why? And most of all, if there is a victim, where is justice and truth for them?*

CHAPTER 19

Andy called Dan and told him of his intention to call Paul and Trisha and set up an appointment to talk to them together. Dan told him he had no problem with him talking with them. He hung up the call with Dan and called Paul.

"Paul, this is Andy Marx."

"Hello, Andy, what can I do for you?" he asked.

"Paul, I was wondering if there is a good time for me to sit down with you and Trisha to try to recount the events of that evening, step by step," Andy said, fighting some of the traffic on Campbell Street that day.

"Sure, I guess so. What time?"

"I was hoping that maybe we can meet at your home in about an hour. Just text me your address and we can meet up, that is if you have the time."

"Sure, Andy. Look, I'll text you my address as soon as I hang up then I will let Trisha know."

Okay, I'll be there in an hour," Andy said, noticing the clouds still dancing all around the sun. In and out and all about, the truth is in there somewhere.

Paul immediately called Trisha.

"Hey, honey. I just wanted to let you know that Andy Marx is coming over to ask some questions. He wanted us both to be there when he comes. Is that okay with you?"

"Well, of course, it is. We need to find out what happened, don't we?" she asked.

"Yes, yes, we do. I'm certain that if we walk this through step by step, I might be able to recall more. I'm missing something and I just can't remember. Look, I'll be home in about thirty minutes, and we can get ready for his visit."

"Paul, everything is going to be all right, isn't it? You know, we've lived for this for so long. I don't doubt you, and, well, I know you're innocent. You would never be capable of doing something like that."

Paul got home in exactly thirty minutes like he told Trisha. She met him at the door and kissed him, just a light peck at first, and then she really kissed him, deeply, passionately, and rubbing her body against him. Once again, Paul was surprised by this. It seems like the circumstances didn't call for such behavior, but Paul shook it off as Trisha just expressing her love for him through this crisis.

"Now, Trish, look, we have to be completely honest with Marx. He's going to ask the tough questions, just answer as honestly as you can and try to recall everything that happened."

"Oh, I will, Paul. There's nothing for us to hide, is there?" she asked, stroking his back and running her nails gently across his back.

"No, there's not. But I have to remember how I got

that cut lip and that black eye. It had to be the wreck, but was it something else? I'm wondering if the person that is trying to blackmail me was there. You know, maybe knocked me out? Is that how it happened?"

"Not saying it couldn't have happened that way," Trisha replied. "More than likely this had to have happened during the wreck, don't you think? The car had minor damage, right? Well, even though I didn't see it, that's what you told me."

"Yes, it did, and I suppose we'll just have to wait for Marx to ask the questions and we'll give him the best answers," Paul said, wishing Marx was not coming for a while. Trisha had made him want her. She had such a special way of doing that lately. He pulled her closer to him and he whispered softly in her ear, "later, Baby, later."

Just then they heard the car drive up. Paul went to look out the window. "Well, it's Marx. Here we go." Paul went to the front door and waved Andy inside.

"Hello, Paul. Sorry we couldn't come up with anything last night, but today I needed to ask you some questions. I'd like to see if you can recall everything that happened the night of the wreck," Andy said, as they went to the living room. Paul motioned to Andy to sit in the recliner while he and Trisha sat on the couch together. Trisha's gaze was intent on Andy Marx, as if she was trying to figure him out. She tried to relax and smile but all she could manage was a weak grin.

"Andy, this is my fiancée, Trisha Dishman, soon to be Trisha Taylor. Trisha, meet Andy Marx," Paul said, as he leaned forward, unable to sit back on the couch.

"It's my pleasure to meet you, sir. Paul has told me a lot about you."

"Thank you. If you don't mind, let's start with the story about the meeting and the wreck, Paul. It's been some weeks, and I need you to recall the events that led to the wreck."

"I'll do my best," Paul said, as he and Trisha sat on the couch together.

"Where were you both that night of the wreck?" Andy asked, looking directly at Trisha, not Paul as he asked the question. Trisha started to speak but thought better of it and held her tongue.

"As I told you, I went to a meeting that night with representatives from Silver Lake. They are the company we have doing the franchising of our brand. The meeting went well, and we did have a few drinks before the meeting."

"Were you sober when you left?" Andy questioned.

"Well, not exactly. I drank more than I thought because I did have a nasty hangover the next day," Paul said, looking at Trisha and then back to Andy.

"So, is it possible you might have blacked out before the collision?"

"No, I couldn't have, there was a bright light in my face, and it blinded me for a second. Then the crash. From there, I can't seem to remember what happened."

"Did you see anyone in the area? You said you were out but then woke up to find your car had been damaged and thought that maybe you hit a deer?"

"Yes, I was sure it had to be something like that. There was minor damage to the right front fender area."

"Where was this crash exactly?" Andy asked, studying Paul and then Trisha as he awaited the answer.

"It was out by an old farmhouse that I think is abandoned just east of town. There was a detour off of Highway 14 that took me by the house, and I could barely make anything out at night as it was very dark. I remember thinking I wondered what the history of the old place was but continued to follow the detour signs.

Funny, I couldn't remember them being there before that day. I go that way to our offices every day.

After I came to and saw the damage, I just thought I hit a deer and that I could get the car fixed and call my insurance guy the next day. I drove home. I guess I drank enough that I knew my head hurt, but I don't remember having a black eye or a cut lip. But Trisha noticed it the next day, didn't you, dear?"

"Well, yes, right before... " she stopped mid-sentence as Paul shot her a look as if to say don't talk about personal stuff. Andy caught Paul's look. "Well, right before we had breakfast," she said, looking for approval from Paul.

"You had already seen the body in the trunk, right? Why didn't you tell Trisha what you saw?"

"I was just trying to keep her out of it," Paul said, looking sheepish and somewhat guilty.

"Paul, that seems odd to me that you didn't tell her. I mean, no offense, but she is your fiancée, maybe that is something she should have known," Andy said, staring hard at Paul.

"Yes, I see where you could think that, but I just didn't want her involved. It was true avoidance on my part. We have worked so hard to get where we are and I just could envision all the bad things that were about to happen," Paul said, knowing he just couldn't give up on this dream. He was finding more and more each day that he was beginning to doubt himself. He was thinking that maybe he did do this after all, and this interview was going south on him quickly. Andy's questions were beginning to feel like he was in an imaginary elevator where the top and sides were closing in on him. He was getting claustrophobic.

"You also told me you went back outside and looked one more time in the trunk. Is that when you found that the body was missing?"

"Yes, I couldn't believe it, no blood, and no trace of anything. You have to believe me, I saw it, the body; it was mangled, beyond recognition." Paul said, his voice starting to escalate with the memory of the body so mangled, it made him vomit. His words were becoming staccato and disrupted.

"Trisha, he said nothing to you about this body at the time?" Andy asked.

"Well, no, he didn't in fact. I noticed his cut lip and black eye before we... well, after we took our showers. I asked him what happened, but he just said it was probably from the wreck. He didn't say anything about a body then," she said, slightly smiling at Andy, which he noted mentally it was strange she smiled at a time when they were being questioned about a serious matter. It was interesting that her answers were cut off, she was leaving out something. There seemed to be something she really wanted to tell but stopped short of saying. Andy wrote it down on his notes and kept on questioning.

"Do you mind if the three of us took a ride out to the scene? I'd like to get a better feel for what you saw, what happened, and what the scenario could have been. Maybe you can explain the setting better to me, Paul, if we are there instead of sitting here in the living room. We can take my car. Is that okay with you, Trisha?" She shifted uneasily in her seat.

"Well, I guess it's okay, that is if you think it will help," Trisha said, looking away and out the window. Suddenly and apparently for no particular reason, she had mentally checked out of the interview. Andy kept questioning and Paul answered.

"Well, that's all for now, let's go on out to the site and see what we can gather," Andy said, standing from his seat in the recliner.

"Trisha, are you ready? Trish... hey Trish," Paul said.

Suddenly Trish came back to the conversation. "Okay, yeah, I'm ready." She said, as Andy kept his keen eye on her, studying her. He couldn't help but feel uneasy about Trisha. She had something there she wasn't talking about, and Andy saw it as a red flag. Andy was good, and once he had a feeling about something, he held onto it like a dog holds on to a bone.

The three of them got in Andy's car together, Andy and Paul in front and Trisha in the back seat. They were headed to the scene that had caused Paul so much difficulty and grief in such a short time. As they drove, he kept thinking of how this one night, a night where he thought everything was coming together, he now thought of as the night when everything was falling apart, would be his ruin.

CHAPTER 20

Arriving at the scene that Paul had described to Andy, the three got out of the car. It was still light enough to see everything very well. Andy had noticed an old farmhouse just about an eighth of a mile back. The scene was very close to the house. Andy took a mental note to himself to see who might own it.

As they looked over the scene, Andy easily found the tree that Paul said he had hit. Andy looked around on the ground, looking for footprints or any other evidence lying loosely on the ground. There didn't seem to be anything that suggested that there was even an accident with a car there at all. In fact, it was almost too clean for an accident to have taken place. There was no blood to be found. If Paul had really hit someone, Andy assumed that any mangled body at this scene would have left some blood somewhere.

It made it especially hard for Andy, because now he could suspect Paul had done this murder elsewhere and made the wreck happen here to throw them off track. On the other hand, Andy thought he could be dealing with some deranged killer that might have all the tracks covered and that this case was going to be much more difficult than he thought.

Suddenly, Andy saw something that caught his trained eye.

"Paul, what color is your car?" Andy asked, bending in closer to the tree to look.

"It's black."

"Look here," he said, pointing to the scuff mark on the tree, "Looks like black paint embedded here in the bare spot on the tree." Andy quickly scraped the paint from the tree to an envelope he had taken from his car.

Paul moved in closer to look. Andy took out his phone and took several photographs of the tree and all the ground around it. "It sure does look like the paint on my car," Paul said, rubbing his facial stubble with his right hand. "So, I'm right. This is where the accident took place."

"Appears that way," Andy said, as he moved to another spot and a different angle. "Which way did the blinding light come from?"

"Over there," Paul said, pointing to the left of the tree about thirty feet and across the road.

Andy walked slowly across the state road. On the other side, he searched the ground again, looking for any clue he could find. There seemed to be nothing there. As he walked back across the gravel road, he stopped and noticed that Trisha was staring at the old, abandoned farmhouse.

"Trisha, do you see something?" Andy asked, startling Trisha. She turned slowly at the sound of his question to face him.

"Oh no, nothing. I was just looking away for a moment."

"You sure?"

"Yes, yes... I'm sure. I was just thinking how complicated that this investigation is and how you seem to be really good at what you do," she said, this time without smiling.

"Well, thank you. Have you ever been here before, Trisha?"

"Uh, no, I haven't, it just seems creepy out here. It is giving me chills. To think that someone could be evil enough to try and hurt Paul and everything he has worked so hard for is just beyond my understanding," she said, turning to look one more time at the old house.

"I understand," Andy said, making a mental note of how Trisha seemed to be captivated by the house much more than the conversation.

"I think I've seen all I need to see here. Let's go back to your place, and I'll drop you two off. There are some other things Mike and I need to do. I need to process what I have seen here and some other interviews to do. It might be a few days before we get back to you."

The three of them got back into Andy's SUV and drove back to Paul and Trisha's house. He let them out in the drive, and he watched them walk slowly inside the house. Andy looked all around the house wondering if someone was watching them. There were woods on the right that would be an easy place to hide and spy on the Taylor house.

Maybe Paul is right, and someone really did watch him and sneak out of the woods to get the body and remove it from the trunk. But this story is so unbelievable; it's hard to buy into this mess. In all reality though, it could have taken place just like Paul said. Mike and I would go back to the crash scene soon, and even look the house over. There's just something about that house that Trisha was right about. There's something real creepy going on and maybe Paul and Trisha are a part of that "real creepy".

Andy drove his vehicle away slowly while trying to peer through the woods that were now on his left and hoping to see something out of place. He saw nothing and started to drive faster as he slowly disappeared from Trisha's sight. Trisha had a worried look on her face.

Chapter 21

Linda Hastings was relieved to see the Kansas City skyline in her rearview mirror. She couldn't believe in a few hours she would be visiting with her best friend, Trisha Dishman, from high school and college. Linda realized that she had to get away from the big city and a job filled with too much pressure, but she didn't want to call Trisha and ask if she could come to Redfield. She thought she would just drive that direction and see Trisha. She couldn't tell Trish what her plans were, when she didn't even know them herself.

Linda pulled off the interstate to get gas and called Trish to see if she could meet for lunch. She dialed the number but got only the voicemail. Linda told Trish she was going through town and wanted to know if they could meet for lunch. She told her that they had lots of catching up to do, and she was excited to meet Paul, the man of Trisha's dreams. After hanging up, Linda wasn't sure a surprise visit was best, but she would soon know.

She didn't plan on telling Trish right away that she had quit her job and was looking for a change of scenery. Linda planned on seeing how the meal and conversation went before she brought up that information. Trish's parents had apartment rentals in Springfield and in Redfield, and Linda was hoping to snag one with some help from her best friend. Trish had always said, "If you ever need anything, let me know"... well, Linda hoped she had meant it.

Arriving in Springfield, Linda called Trisha to let her know that she was in town and wanted to meet for lunch.

"Hello Trish, this is Linda Hastings. I just got into town and thought maybe we could meet for lunch," Linda said, pulling over into a parking area to talk.

"Sure, that sounds good. It's been so long, I almost forgot what you looked like. Why don't you take a picture of yourself and send it to me? I bet you haven't changed a bit."

"Well, I have changed since high school and college. Life hasn't always been kind. But I bet you're as pretty as I remember you last time I came to town," Linda said.

"Awe, Linda, you were always so kind. I'll meet you at noon at Paul's restaurant downtown. Then we can head to the mall and shop if you like."

"Sounds good. I'll be there at noon."

Linda took a selfie and forwarded it to her friend. A funny request, she thought, but no matter, she was just probably curious. It had been a little while since she visited.

After their luncheon with lots of conversation catching up on each other's lives, Linda and Trisha went shopping at the mall. Trisha was trying to enjoy what Linda recalled about how her mom took her shopping when she was little and that she wanted to go back and see her mom sometime soon.

Trisha's thoughts were interrupted by seeing a man she knew walking towards them at a distance. Trisha knew she had to avoid the man, so she pulled Linda with her into the bath and body shop.

"What are you doing?" Linda asked, as they hurried together into the shop.

"Nothing, nothing at all. I just saw someone I need to avoid. Just one of Paul's friends that I'd rather not talk to right now."

"Oh, I see. Okay, but that sounds either mysterious or the guy has hit on you before and you didn't care for him," Linda said, with a wink.

"It's not like that at all; it's just one of Paul's business partners. Quick! Turn around and don't let him see you."

They both turned, but Linda looked over her shoulder as Ted Jansen walked by. Trisha looked over her left shoulder and saw that he had walked past.

"Whew! That was close. I just didn't want to talk to the guy," Trisha said, looking worried.

"I don't know why not. He's really kind of cute," Linda said, following his walk as he strode confidently down the mall.

"Don't worry about him, Linda. The guy is married," Trisha said, as she looked at her phone. It was getting late. "Look, Linda, I have to go now. I have to get back home, or Paul will shoot me."

"I get it. I am staying at a local motel for a couple of days. I will have to start looking for an apartment tomorrow as I have one in mind. It shouldn't take long for the movers to get down here after I close the deal," Linda said, smiling. "Thanks for meeting me. We always had fun together. I can't wait to meet Paul."

"Don't look for an apartment until I check with Dad and Mom about some of their rental properties to see if one is available."

They walked out of the mall and headed to Trisha's vehicle. Trisha opened the door and got in her Escalade, starting the motor and turning down the radio. She slowly pulled out of her parking space and thought of what she had said to Linda. "I have to get back home, or Paul will shoot me." *Oh yeah, how many times do people say that? Yeah, I got to get home, my husband will shoot me. Of course, that's not what they meant. But with this thing with Paul, I'm starting to worry....*

Katy was worried about her pregnancy. She was also starting to worry about how involved the case was getting. Both of those thoughts made her nervous and during her first pregnancy, being thirty-six years old, she would want to have some tests done to make sure that everything went well.

Mike and she had an appointment to look into her family background and DNA work to see if there were any serious diseases or complications in her family history. She sent off for a DNA history and genealogical review. She hoped to gain some good information that she could give her doctors. She thought the information might arrive soon.

Katy wished she could discuss this all with Mike. But he had gone out with Andy to interview a few people. She wanted him to be safe, and she didn't want to worry about him chasing down criminals. She was worried that this one case could get like the old Allison Branch case.

She shivered at the thought, but Katy had become a much stronger woman. Her views were more tough-minded. Somehow, she knew deep down that Allison Branch was not a rarity. There would be more just like Allison Branch to deal with. Katy knew the horror of someone like Branch first-hand. She was just hoping that things could be passed off to the police. She wanted this baby. She needed this baby. Lately, things had gone so right for her and Mike. She looked up to the sky and muttered to herself, *"Please God, please we need this to happen for us. Please protect our baby and my husband."*

Andy and Mike were on their way to Lee Hamlin's restaurant. They needed some answers from him and both of them were highly suspicious of Lee. It had come down to the thought that either Paul or Lee was the top suspect, but which one was guilty? They had already interviewed Ted Jansen, Paul's partner, and they could find nothing there, at least not for the moment.

Paul had told Ted that he would be interviewed and what the incident was all about. Ted would keep the secret. He was a loyal partner in the business, and he understood the dangers of what this could mean for the company. Paul's opportunity was also Ted's. According to Andy's interviews, Ted was clean as a whistle.

Andy and Mike drove up to the restaurant, parked the car and went inside Northside Burger Emporium. They gave the young hostess their card, and she went to talk to the manager. The manager looked at the card and then disappeared into the back to talk to Lee.

"Hey, Lee, there's two guys out front that want to talk with you. Card says they're from M & M Private Investigators."

"Okay, tell them I'll be out in a minute," Lee knew that this day would happen. He had to gather himself a bit and make sure he knew what he would say. He had rehearsed it for some time now. This part was hard, but he told himself to talk slow and remain calm.

He raised both hands to his temples, rubbing them to try to stop the image. It was the bloody image of a body put into the back of Paul's car. All right, gather yourself, relax and don't panic. *Put those images out of your mind. You're a successful businessman, poised, confident, and reassured. You can't let them see you sweat.*

Lee rose from his desk, shaking the image of the bloody and mangled body from his mind. He took a deep breath and strode as confidently as he could out to meet the investigators who were destroying his plan. *Calm, be calm, now.*

"I'm Lee Hamlin. I understand from my manager you want to speak to me?"

"Yes, I'm Andy Marx and this is my partner, Mike Parsons. We'd like to ask you a few questions about Paul Taylor, if you don't mind."

"Of course not. Please follow me back to a more private room," Lee said, as he walked towards the back of the restaurant and led them into the room that was used for private parties. He motioned for them to be seated at a four-top table right inside the door. They sat down and he slid into a chair across from them. He studied their faces trying to measure each man, but Andy quickly started the questioning.

"We'll get right to the issue, Mr. Hamlin," Andy said, opening his notebook. "We're not cops. We work for ourselves investigating incidents for clients. Paul Taylor is one of our clients. How well do you know Paul?"

"I've known him since high school. I moved back to

Redfield from Spokane when my mom passed away. I basically lived on my own when I came back. Paul and I were friends in high school. He always was a good athlete, had plenty of friends, and always had the best girlfriends," Lee said, without smiling, something that caught Andy's attention. "I see him at Chamber of Commerce meetings a lot."

"It seems like Paul Taylor is doing pretty well in town. Looks like his expansion is going well. How much do you know about his business?"

Lee grinned, knowing that this was a trick question that he already had an answer for. "He's doing well. Word on the street is he's going to expand in franchising. Don't know how much of that is true, but I wish him luck in his endeavors," Lee said, his gut turning on the inside making that statement. *Of course, I don't wish that shithead luck. I just have to say that. Be calm, be calm, Lee. Bloody image. Go away. Stop it.* Lee smiled and said, "So, if it happens, I'll be happy for him."

Andy was writing a couple of notes.

"Can you tell me where you were on the night of April 14th?" Andy asked.

"Sure, I was at my restaurant until closing. My manager can tell you I was there because we had to discuss some staffing issues."

"Is there anything else you can tell us about Paul? Were there any problems between you two in the past?" Mike asked. Andy stared hard at Lee and leaned in closer across the table. He had a purpose in doing this.

"N-n-no. There's n-nothing else," Lee replied.

The men stood and shook hands. Lee quickly retreated to the back office, and Andy and Mike left the restaurant after the strange and revealing interview. They walked slowly to the car, Andy turning to look back at the restaurant. He was thinking something that

Mike didn't know. Mike was curious to find out what was on Andy's mind.

They got back inside the car and started to leave the parking lot. Andy looked thoughtful and turned to Mike. "There's something there. Two things here, partner. One, we need to question his manager, and, two, we need more research on Lee. He has some problems in his past. Did you notice his speaking slowly and then the stuttering?"

"I did. Where was that coming from?"

"He had to rehearse what he was going to say. He was going too fast, and he was starting to stutter. I know that because I had a teacher that helped me with the same thing. I'm pretty much over it now, but I had a problem with it in grade school. She would tell me that if I would slow down my speech, I would stutter less and less. He has something going on inside that head of his. He was moving too fast."

"I saw you note something else when he was talking about girlfriends. What was that?"

"He didn't smile," Andy answered. "He actually grimaced. That was not a good sign. Most guys grin or smile when they speak of high school and old girlfriends. They don't grimace."

Mike just nodded, wondering how he caught those things. *The same way you notice how you know a criminal is lying on the stand. Observation, just plain observation and gut feelings. Interesting how Marx and I are different, but really the same. Yep, Lee's a problem.*

They drove the rest of the way to the office in silence. It was already the first of June, and the Missouri humidity was about to take its rightful place in the summer.

Back inside his office, Lee Hamlin knew he could no longer stay at work. He told the manager that he had to run a few errands, and that he would be back in a few hours. He left the building and drove to the farmhouse where he immediately dialed his phone.

"Hey, this is Lee. I've got problems. I know I said I wouldn't bother you again, but this is very important.

CHAPTER 22

Lee hung up the call and started to pace the floor of the old farmhouse. He could not believe that they were trying to put pressure on him. He was not the one to pressure. They would find out soon that pressuring him would be a mistake.

Lee went to the back and got the key to the freezer. He walked outside, slowly placed the key in the lock, and turned the key until the latch came apart with a click. He took the lock off and gently opened the lid...

There she was. He peered closely and saw his mangled and bloody victim, now frozen stiff and sporting a pale blue color, staring back at him with a face he could not have recognized if he tried. But he did know her. She was easy to kidnap, a plan that was working perfectly until those two investigators got in the way.

Lee thought back to that day and all that had happened. He wanted to get to Paul Taylor, and this was the perfect way. Set him up and then make him pay. Blackmail. The dead body, well, that was just from rage. His uncontrollable rage had assisted him in this kill.

How easy it was to kidnap her, place her in the trunk, and drive her to the old farmhouse. I took her to the woods behind the property, bound and gagged. I wanted to have mercy on her, but I could feel the rage building inside me. I had to mangle that face, the one that rejected me years ago. I looked at her bulging eyes that showed fear and that begged me to please let her go. The tears, oh, the tears running down her face like a river. Those tears became very satisfying to me, didn't they? Should I take the gag off just to hear her scream? I decided to leave her gagged. No use letting anyone possibly hear her. Oh no, they would be muffled, and they wouldn't last long.

I saw the crowbar coming down on her head. The first blow crushed her head, and she began to shake and shiver in a convulsive state. I continued to bring the crowbar up and then down, continuously and mercilessly, beating her face beyond all recognition. She was quite dead then, and I had finally stopped, exhausted from my rage. My rage lessened as I calmed my breathing and closed my eyes for a minute.

I then brought the body back to the farmhouse and placed it in the freezer until I could execute part two of my plan. And, of course, there was a part two.

Lee slammed the lid with force, and it bounced a couple of times before he finally closed it more gently so it caught. He put the lock back on and hid the key where he usually kept it, in a coffee can in the cabinet above the stove.

—▲—

Paul was home with Trisha now, and he couldn't

forget the scene that had started this incident. He thought of how Trisha was staring at the farmhouse, and he sensed that it had made her act so strangely. Trish was telling Paul of her lunch with Linda Hastings. Paul remembered Linda, but was only half listening as his mind kept drifting to the scene.

"Trish, when we were out at the scene, I remember Marx asking you what you were looking at. Well, what was it?"

"It was nothing, Paul. The old house was just reminding me of a dream that I had. Really, honey, it was nothing. I was just thinking that the old house was creepy."

"Come over and sit by me, Trisha. Your parents will be here soon for their visit. It will be nice to have them here for a few days, but I wish we could spend some time alone."

Trisha smiled at Paul and felt the sudden urge to have sex with him. But she knew they didn't have the time before her parents came. They would be there shortly. She rubbed the back of his neck and purred softly, "Soon, my dear, very soon. We'll have to be quiet with them here, but I need you."

Normally, Trish would have been going over the house, making sure everything was just right, and there wasn't a speck of dust in the place. But she seemed very relaxed as she leaned into him and kissed his neck. Paul began to feel the same urges as Trisha, but as luck would have it, at that moment, Trisha's parents pulled up in the driveway.

Paul went out the door first and Trisha followed. Rich and Carol Dishman got out of their SUV and smiled broadly as Trisha hugged Carol first and then Rich. She told them how happy she was to see them and that they were looking forward to enjoying their stay.

"Oh, Mom and Dad, please come in and we'll get

your things put away," Trisha said.

They put their things in the spare floor level bedroom. That is where they always stayed when they came to visit. Her parents had settled in and unloaded their suitcases and the four of them headed out to sit on the patio with a cup of coffee in hand.

"We're so glad you came," Trisha said. "There is so much we have to tell you."

CHAPTER 23

The conversation had been mostly about Paul's new business venture and about the opportunity that Paul had in his grasp. The hard part was going to be how Paul could tell the story of a missing body he found in his trunk to his future in-laws. This would be tough because like most parents, the Dishmans would think of protecting their daughter first. For them to believe Paul and his story, they were going to have to have a lot of faith in Paul as a person and also faith in their daughter's judgment in picking him. It made Paul extremely nervous. One thing he did know, being up front with the parents of his future bride was a must, and it wasn't Trisha's job to tell the story. It was his.

"Look, Rich and Carol, there's something that I have to tell you. We're so glad you came down to visit, but something happened some weeks ago that you should know about," Paul said, swallowing hard and taking a deep breath. "I want you to know this up front and don't feel that we, well, that I, should keep this from you."

Carol sat up straight in her chair leaning towards Paul and shifting a quizzical glance at Trisha.

"You see, I'm on the verge of having my business branch out now, and I have an equity firm controlling the market for me. This is huge and the gold mine I have been looking for. But back on April 14, something happened that shocked us and, yet, it has been a mystery ever since."

"I came back from the meeting with the equity firm that night. I'd been drinking and took a detour from the road they were apparently fixing. I hit something on that road and somehow, I blacked out. I don't think it was from the drinks, but from hitting a tree. I came home with a cut lip and black eye. I went out to the garage to look at the possible damage to my car, and then I noticed that the trunk was slightly open. I carefully lifted the trunk and saw a bloody, dead body in my car. I was shocked," Paul said, noticing the looks on Rich and Carol's faces. "I threw up in the garage and closed the lid of the trunk."

"Oh, my word," said Carol. "Did you call the police?"

"Oh no, it gets worse, Carol," Paul said. He looked to Trisha for support, but she wasn't willing to offer any. "So, I went inside after cleaning up the mess and then Trisha and I, well... we... talked about what had happened, and she did notice the cut on my lip and the black eye. I was recalling the wreck from the night before. I started to wonder if I had actually run over a body by accident. I never saw anything that looked like a body, but only a flash of light."

"I went back out to the garage, thinking that maybe I did drink too much and had some kind of wild illusion about the body. I carefully opened the trunk, but the body was gone. I was in shock, I was sure I saw a body, but now I was thinking it was just from drinking too much."

"Paul, this sounds kind of crazy. Maybe it was that you were just imagining it," Rich said, looking warily at Paul and shifting his gaze to Trisha. Trisha was looking out the window, seemingly disengaged from the conversation. "Trisha...Trisha!" Rich said, trying to bring his daughter back to the conversation. She suddenly focused her eyes on her father.

"I'm sorry, Dad, I was just remembering all we have been through up to this point," Trisha said, taking a drink of her coffee with her left hand. Carol looked at her, seeming confused.

"Honey, you are holding your cup with your left hand. You're right-handed," Carol said.

"Oh, Mom, I hurt my wrist the other day lifting the table to put a coaster underneath. It's nothing really, but it just hurts a little. I'm just trying to let it heal."

"Oh, I see," Carol said. "Well, anyway, I'm sorry, Paul, for interrupting you. Go on."

Paul had not noticed Trisha using her left hand more. He felt embarrassed that he had missed something like that, but the incidents in his life seemed to be bogging him down. He was paying more attention to his own situation than his fiancée. He continued.

"I went to the body shop to get the car fixed and later the owner of the shop found a note on my car. The note was asking for ten thousand dollars and that they knew what I did and where the body was. I know at that moment I should have gone to the police, but I just didn't because of what had happened before. I know you remember that incident, Rich and Carol." They both shook their heads in agreement.

"I just thought the cops wouldn't give me a break. I thought they would push the envelope much harder. So, I went to private investigators. One of them is a friend of my dad's and served in the military with him."

"Are they getting anywhere?" Rich asked, seeming to be more concerned by the minute.

"They have been questioning people," Paul said, looking for his future in-laws' understanding. "I think they will get somewhere. I know my dad thinks so."

"Well, be sure to keep us posted," Carol said. "This seems so incredible."

"Mom, it's going to be fine. Paul and his father trust these guys. I think they know what they are doing. Should we go inside?"

Paul opened the screen door and let them all go before him. He felt better after he told them, but he still wondered what they were thinking now and wished he could hear their conversation when they went to their bedroom for the night. What exactly were they thinking of their future son-in-law?

Paul had showered and lay on his bed, watching the ceiling fan blades spin around, hypnotizing him for a second. He couldn't believe his life was crumbling, falling apart in such a short time. This issue had to be solved.

Trisha walked out of her shower and into the bedroom with only her towel on. She dropped the towel to the floor and lay down beside Paul. She ran her fingers across his smooth, shaven chest. Paul was starting to feel her soft skin, rubbing up against his body and he began to breathe harder. She kissed his cheek and then his neck, slowly building the excitement in Paul.

Quickly she was on top of him, and she made love to him, madly, passionately until they both fell on their sides of the bed, exhausted, trying hard to catch their breath.

As soon as he began to breathe more normally, Paul drew Trisha close to him and kissed her on the lips. Trisha and he had never made love before when her parents visited.

"That was so good, my love," Trisha said, as she snuggled up close to Paul. "A bit daring and exciting, don't you think?"

"Definitely," Paul said, smiling at Trisha. "I can't remember ever doing that with your parents here."

"We haven't, but there is always a first time for everything. Something new, something thrilling is always around the corner for you, my love. I'm going to make you very, very happy in every way. I love you."

"I love you, too," Paul said, thinking this must be a dream. His fiancée had morphed into a creative sexual being. Something so different. It was mysterious to him in so many ways, yet so exciting and thrilling in others. It just didn't fit their dilemma. But Paul was not complaining. He just couldn't figure out why. He just figured she was blossoming into a wife she wanted to be.

This story is so bizarre. Is this only the beginning of my troubles? I have worked so hard; my future wife is beautiful, and the business is about to become everything I hoped it would. Then this happens. A body in my trunk, private investigators, unknown suspects. Who is behind this? Or is it really me? Is my future wife making love to a killer? I have to be positive, but slowly, I'm beginning to think that maybe I did do it. Life will come crashing down, the business in the crapper, no wife, as she will leave me for sure. Where the hell am I? This just can't happen. Not now.

Paul drifted off to sleep and the dreams would not be good. It was usually the same dream over and over: the bloody, mangled body and an empty trunk. He always woke up in a sweat.

Lee had gained a new manager a couple of months ago. His name was John Restor. John was easy to hire as he was fired from the competition, Taylor's Brew House, Inc. John was a full partner at Taylor's until the day he was let go. The events that led up to his dismissal were quite corrupt and ugly.

John had skimmed funds from the company. Paul had noticed that the bottom lines were unusually low for a few months. It was easy to do as John had the responsibility of auditing funds for each location; a rooster in the henhouse so to speak. After an independent audit was done, John was found guilty of writing himself bonuses, using company money for Christmas presents and fine fancy things for his bride.

Needless to say, John was fired and had to make restitution to Taylor's Brew House. Part of the settlement that was reached out of court gave John his share of his initial investments, and he was free to seek employment elsewhere without having a bad reference follow him. That's where Lee Hamlin came into the picture with employment for John and plans to use him for his own benefit.

John's settlement gave Lee some cash infusion for his business, and he offered a form of future partnership for John if he did Lee these favors. All he had to do was a few nefarious things that had Paul Taylor as a target. John was more than willing to do these "favors" for Lee because Paul Taylor would be ruined. John would be back on top in the business world, and the thought of Paul Taylor's demise and spending time in jail was very palatable to John Restor.

Lee had plans for John Restor. Those plans would

take John to a world he never thought he would see. Oh, but he would see all sides of that world. He would see it not only as a manager in Lee's restaurant but as someone who owed Lee a few favors for taking him in with the potential to be a partner someday.

CHAPTER 24

Lee Hamlin was beginning to boil. He had a few things left for John to take care of for him and one was an alibi. John was listening on the other end of the phone call.

"John, I need a favor. The private investigators I asked you to follow want to ask you some questions about my whereabouts on the night of Paul's wreck. I need you to tell them I was working with you that night as we were short staffed."

"I can do that," John replied, thinking of how that would make his old partner look bad.

"Be sure you don't get weak and don't cave to them. Andy Marx is a tough son of a bitch, and he won't give up. Just stay on point."

"I will, don't worry. I want this frame up just as bad as you," John said.

"After that gets done, then I will have just one more job for you and then we can say goodbye to Paul Taylor for good," Lee said, feeling somewhat giddy over that proposition. "They'll probably be there today, so be ready. Just call me when they are done. I want to know what they say."

Lee disconnected his call to John. He was feeling more comfortable all the time. He knew John would protect him. There were getting to be too many variables, though, and this was getting harder, even for his diabolical mind. It was time to do one more thing to muddy the old waters just a bit and make life for that no-paying asshole Paul Taylor miserable.

Lee took out a pair of rubber gloves and a clean sheet of paper he hadn't touched. He began to write the note. When he was finished, he wet the envelope with a small sponge. He then sealed the envelope and addressed it to the Redfield Police Department.

He took the letter and got into his car, drove to a local drop mailbox, and deposited the letter. He had done it. He was tired of not getting paid and when the police got this letter, they would surely arrest Paul. Lee felt good about himself for the first time in a while. He was way ahead of Paul and the private investigators. Lee thought himself to be quite the genius at this point. He was going to have Paul exactly where he wanted him. In jail.

Mike and Andy were at the office. Katy was in the back working on the books. Andy had solved the old grandpa kidnapping case.

"The old man had taken the kid and was hiding out in an old, abandoned motel. He was making plans to take the kid and go out of the country but came up short financially to make it happen," Marx said, looking at his notes in the file. "It was easy to find him as he left a trail from the video at the bank. I checked it and got the plates from the car. Then I called my friend. It was his, all right. Cops followed it to the point of arrest. I guess the old man will have to explain that one in court. I might have to testify in that one."

"Well, you did great once again, buddy. But what's up with the Paul Taylor case? What's on your mind?" Mike inquired.

"Mike, I think we need to check out Lee's alibi. Somehow, I think if we check with the manager, we might find out something different. Let's head on over there and see what we find."

"All right, let's go. I'll tell Katy to watch the front of the office."

Mike went back and saw his lovely wife Katy, working the files of recent cases and updating the financials. She was looking more beautiful every day, and her pregnancy was making her glow. She looked up at him and smiled.

"Need something, mister?" she asked.

"Just you, Baby. Nothing else, just you."

He walked over and kissed her cheek. "Andy and I are going to question the manager at Lee's restaurant. Andy doesn't believe Lee's alibi."

"Mike, be careful. We have so much good happening for us. I just want you to be careful," Katy said, giving Mike a pouty look.

"You know I will. I can't wait to find out what we are having."

"I guess it's the thing to do nowadays. I kind of wish we would just look at it as a surprise and not know," Katy said. "I think it would be fun."

"I'll think about that," Mike said. "I'll do whatever you'd like."

"Let's be a little old-fashioned here. Let's try not to know. We tell the doctor we would rather not know the sex of the baby. What do you think?"

"Okay, I'm in," Mike said, kissing her cheek once more. "We'll be back shortly. Do you think you can watch the front of the office for us while we're gone? Cases are starting to come in, and we don't want to miss any in our beginning stages."

"Sure thing, if you give me a good kiss when we get home, not these little pecks on the cheek."

"See you soon, Mrs. Parsons," Mike said, winking and feeling like a million bucks. *This girl, this woman, well, she makes my world better.*

Mike headed out the door, and Katy began to wonder if this private investigation thing was ever going to be the safe, secure job that Mike needed. She relented to knowing that every case had the potential to be dangerous. Her intuition was telling her that this case was much more dangerous than it was thought to be at the beginning. She began to slip back into some of her old ways of thinking. She was beginning to fear for Mike, and much more, for herself, now that she was carrying a child. This child that she wanted with all her being, well, she had to have it and Mike needed to be there, to be the father she knew he could be. She said a silent prayer asking for his and her safety and, especially, the safety of her unborn child. *Please, God, don't put the three of us in harm's way. Protect us, please....*

Mike and Andy arrived at Lee's restaurant a little after noon. The place was busy, but they asked for the manager anyway. Soon, John Restor appeared.

"What can I do for you gentlemen?" John asked. "I'm John Restor, the manager."

"I'm Andy Marx, private investigator with M & M Private Investigators. This is my partner, Mike

Parsons. We'd like to ask you a few questions if you don't mind."

"No, not at all. Follow me back to my office and we can talk there."

They went towards the back through the swinging doors and headed to a small, cramped office. There were only three chairs; two were on the other side of the boss's seat that John offered to Mike and Andy. The other was Lee's chair, in which John sat, facing the two men.

"So, what is it that you would like to ask me?"

Andy started. "On the night of April 14, a couple months back, what were you doing?"

John looked at his phone calendar. "I was working. I haven't had a day off in two months," John replied, remaining calm.

"Was Lee Hamlin working that night?"

"Yes, we were very short on staff that night, and, when that happens, sometimes we both have to work. I went home early as he gave me a break, and he closed for me."

"I see. So, what time did Lee come in to help?"

"Well, it was around ten or ten-thirty. I can't remember exactly."

"What time did you leave, Mr. Restor?" Mike asked.

"Around midnight, I think."

"When do you usually get done closing?

"Usually, we are done around one-thirty or two."

"Mr. Restor, were there any other employees working with Lee late that night?"

"I'm not sure who stayed. I guess you would have to ask Lee."

Mike got the feeling, by that answer, that any good manager would have known who else had to close. John didn't really have to answer that or hand over any employee information he might have on record. There was no subpoena. Still, Mike was thinking that there had to be one more person they could interview. But, which one?

"Mr. Restor, thanks for your time, and I hope we don't need to bother you again," Andy said, knowing in his mind that Restor had been smooth with his answers. Not knowing who was helping to close for the evening was a big mistake for a manager. Andy knew it, and he knew they would be back to question this guy. Soon.

CHAPTER 25

John quickly dialed Lee after Mike and Andy left. He began by saying that the question asked that would have to be covered up was who else was working that night.

"I don't want to ruin your alibi, Lee, but if these nosy investigators asked for a work schedule, I'll just have to go back and eliminate the one we had scheduled on the computer for that day."

"I see. What did you tell them?"

"I told them we were short on help and that you came in to help close with me around ten. I told them I can't remember if anyone was working with you at close, but we can cover that up. They were pretty sly. I don't know how to get these guys off your trail, but I have been through some rough questioning just from Paul Taylor's partners. These guys are much tougher."

"Listen, I have a plan to throw them off for a while. A letter I sent to the cops should take care of it. I already dropped the letter off. As soon as they read that, they will be all over him. Paul will be their main interest and, most likely, the main suspect of a murder. They will be pressing him while we get away with it all."

"Okay, but these two guys, Mike and Andy, they are looking at us hard. I could tell they were thinking way ahead of my answers, and we need to be careful. I don't need another setback like I had with Taylor's Brew House."

"I got you covered, John. You just leave the rest to me."

Andy drove and Mike looked at the traffic fly by on Highway 13 as they headed back to the office.

"You believe the guy?" Mike asked, glancing over at Andy for a response.

"No, but right now, we need one more interview. One that is outside the circle we've been interviewing. We don't seem to be getting the break we need."

"I think Lee's guilty, no doubt. John even looks like the guilty type, too, sneaky and suspicious. Lee's nervous as hell," Mike said, rubbing his forehead from the headache he felt as he sifted through the two interview scenes in his mind.

"They may be nervous, but we haven't found any proof that they are guilty of anything yet."

"Look, Andy, what does your gut say? You have always had the gut feeling, the intuition. Is he our guy or is it Paul? Like I said before, don't leave Paul out."

Andy looked over at Mike, not exactly with surprise, and said, "I'm not leaving Paul out."

They drove on in silence. Andy was going through the file in his mind and Mike was going through the one on his lap.

Ken Satterfield has been a police officer in Redfield for twenty years. He was mostly a fair and unbiased cop who did his job by the books. Corruption in a police force could be a problem for any city, but Ken seemed to stay above it. There were a few cops on the city's force he was wary of, but he had risen above the rest to become Chief of Police and had fought against bad cops his whole career.

He shuffled the letter around, touching it with only his hands that were covered with rubber gloves. He looked up at Cory Blackwell, then back down to the letter, raising his eyebrows.

"When did you receive this letter?" Satterfield asked.

"Just this morning, sir. I documented the time received. I have been careful not to contaminate the letter," Blackwell said.

"You know the name of the guy mentioned in this anonymous letter is high profile, right?"

"Yes, sir, I do."

"Did you work on the last case we had with Paul Taylor? You know, the case where he was accused of harassment?"

"I did, sir."

"And you do remember how wrong we got that case?"

"Yes, sir."

"When an anonymous letter talks about mangled bodies, murder, and hidden corpses, we still have to check it out. I'm not sure how much of this is truth or fiction. We don't have a weapon, body, or motive, or even a missing person's report. Pretty slim outside of this letter."

"I know, Chief, but do you want me to bring him in for questioning at least? I feel it deserves that much."

"You're right, it does. Go ahead and see if he will

come in."

"What about a search warrant?" Blackwell asked.

"Don't think we have that kind of information as of yet. Remember, suspects are innocent until proven guilty, and we need reasonable cause for the search warrant. Don't think we are there yet. Give him a call and see if he will come in voluntarily and remind him it is for his protection as well. Keep me informed on this."

"Yes, sir." Blackwell said, turning and walking out of the chief's office. Remembering he had dealt with Paul Taylor before and he wasn't successful last time, but this time, well, he couldn't wait to get started.

Paul got the call from Officer Cory Blackwell at two o'clock in the afternoon. He wasn't in the mood for this at all, not today, not ever. He got weak in the knees when the voice on the other end was Cory Blackwell. Cory had worked the case before when Paul was accused of harassment. He seemed to want to get Paul for some reason, and Paul was lucky that he got out of the last predicament with the cops. If it wasn't for the good lawyer his dad found for him and Paul's honesty, he would probably have served some jail time or at least been on probation.

That good lawyer passed away a year ago, and now Paul felt like he needed to call his dad as he felt cornered now and didn't know which way he should turn. He wanted to go outside his office, get in his car, and drive as far away from this town as he could. But he couldn't give up, not now. He shut the door to his office and quietly spoke on the phone.

"What's this all about?"

"Well, we received an anonymous letter, stating

some pretty damaging things about you. We thought it best if you could come in and answer a few questions," Blackwell said.

Paul hesitated, and then answered, "I think I'd like to have a lawyer present. I'm not guilty of anything, and I will talk to you. But I want an attorney present, whether you are charging me with anything or not."

"Can you make it to the station by four this afternoon?"

"Why don't you give me your number, and I'll call you back."

"That's fine," Blackwell replied, before giving the number to Paul.

Paul hung up and immediately called his dad. "Dad, the cops seem to have an anonymous letter, accusing me of things I didn't do or know anything about."

"Slow down, son. Which cops?" Dan asked, through his pursed lips.

"It's Blackwell again. You remember him from the last time. He seems to want to get me. He was on a mission then, and I am sure he will be on that same mission again. He wants to talk with me and ask a few questions at four o'clock. I told him I wanted an attorney present. The guy we used last time is dead, and I don't know what to do."

"Let me call Andy and see if Mike will help us out with this one. Don't agree to anything until I call you back."

"Okay, Dad."

Paul hung up. His legs felt like lead, and his heart was pounding much faster than normal. His mouth was dry and beads of sweat began to form on his upper lip. He felt he would pass out and he was much too young to be having a heart attack, yet he felt like he had all the symptoms.

What the hell is going on? Who is doing this? I need

answers before everything I worked for slips right through my fingers. I'm not a killer, I couldn't be... or am I?

Ted Jansen knocked on the door and asked if he could come in. He had something he wanted to share about payroll at the Springfield location.

"Come in," Paul said, remaining in his chair.

"You okay, Paul? You don't look so good, Buddy."

"Yeah, I'm okay; just a little stress is all. Trying to manage a lot of things at once."

"You need to go home?"

"I might. I'm not feeling the best."

"Well, I just came in to tell you that we might need to add some payroll and hire a few people at the Springfield site. Are you okay with that?"

"Sure, Ted. That's fine. Could you handle it, though? I think I am going to go home for the day."

"No problem," Ted said, as he turned to leave Paul's office. "You get some rest, Paul."

"I'll see you tomorrow, Ted."

Paul was driving slowly towards his house, hardly noticing the stop lights or the cars around him. Everything was a blur of confusion. This letter, from whom he did not know, was quickly becoming a problem. He was starting to feel like whoever was trying to blackmail him was now trying to land him a spot in jail. He could hardly keep his shit together any longer. He felt intense pressure around his temples making sharp, shooting pains go to his head. He was about to break. That just couldn't happen. He promised Trisha that he would make it big, hell, he promised himself the same thing.

As the cars continued to pass him in black and white,

Paul could feel himself slipping down the slippery slope he hoped to avoid. He dreamed in black and white, and now his dreams were starting to become reality. Now, more than ever, he was feeling that he was some kind of monster, that maybe he had gone crazy. This just couldn't be happening. All things in his world are colorless and dull. It was like an old black and white movie where the bad guy was on the run and had some crazy amnesia where he couldn't remember all the atrocities he had committed.

He drove into the garage and put the car in park, trying to come up with some story that sounded plausible. Some kind of story that would get him off this terribly sharp hook he was on, his feet dangling in the air. He told himself three or four versions, none of which seemed to make sense to even him. Paul Taylor was in deep trouble.

Chapter 26

Dan Taylor called Andy Marx. Dan was fidgety and worried about Paul's predicament.

"Hello, Andy, this is Dan. Looks like Paul is in some kind of trouble. Seems like the police received an anonymous letter that may point the finger at him. They have asked him to come in for questioning. They want him to be there by four o'clock."

"Tell him not to go in without a lawyer."

"I was wondering if I could ask Mike to be his lawyer and represent him."

"Not sure what he will say, Dan. Mike has been a prosecutor, not a defense lawyer, and he will want all the information from Paul before he goes and talks with the police. Let me transfer you to Mike's desk. I can't answer for him. Hold just a second." Andy pushed Mike's extension and hung up.

"Hello, this is Dan Taylor."

"Hello, Dan, what can I do for you?"

"Well, it's about Paul and he needs someone to

represent him. Looks like the local police want to bring him in for questioning. They have received an anonymous note that points the finger at Paul and a missing body."

"Well, I have been a prosecutor most of my career, but I know what to do as a defense attorney. You know, I'll have to charge an additional fee on top of the one you're paying the firm."

"Of course," Dan replied, shifting in his seat and worried about the time. "They want him there by four this afternoon."

"Tell Paul to call back and say he will make it by five. Paul needs to come by here right now. I will talk to him, I'm not sure if I can represent him until I get everything from him and I mean everything. There just can't be any surprises. Investigators are too good, and people will find out things if the truth isn't told from the beginning."

"I understand. I will get Paul over there to you. We'll talk then."

Mike hung up and walked into Andy's office. He was not sure what he was going to do. He had thought of Paul being guilty all along, but to represent Paul, he would have to believe in Paul's innocence.

"Andy, I'm not sure about representing Paul. He and Dan will be here shortly, and I have to ask you one more time, do you think he's really innocent?"

"I've known Dan for a long time, and I know this, if he didn't believe it, then I would worry. I think Dan believes his son is innocent, and I have to go with that for now."

"You know this complicates matters. We still need to process John's interview and alibi for Lee Hamlin."

"Mike, I know you're a bit leery of this but try to trust me on this one. I think the guy is innocent. Let me work on the alibi story, and you help Paul out with the cops.

This is a crucial point for Paul. You and I both know there are bad cops out there, and they will do anything to put someone away they don't like. I'm asking as a friend that you help Paul and Dan out here."

"Huge risk, my friend."

"How so?"

"Don't want to lose my license that I worked so hard to gain back."

"I understand that. Listen, I have a strong feeling about Lee and John. They are guilty of something and possibly even the murder and getting rid of the dead body. Besides, I think they had something to do with Paul's car accident. There's more to this than we know."

"Okay, I'll do it, but I'm making sure we play by my rules."

"In the legal realm, you're the boss," Andy said, smiling and getting up from his chair. "I'm going to grab a bite and then come back to the office. If you're here when I get back, we'll discuss the conference. If not, I'll catch up to you later."

Mike got up from the chair in Andy's office, walked down the hall, and sat down behind his new desk. He was deep in thought. *The conundrum. Here it is: If I interview Paul and he looks guilty, I have every right to turn the case down. What is Katy going to say and how will this involve me in ways she doesn't want me to be? I have to think quickly and ask all the right questions, but I have to agree with Andy. There's something about this that is getting more dangerous, and I don't think Paul is guilty. I don't necessarily want to jump to that conclusion without asking the right questions.*

Mike looked straight ahead and saw the picture of Katy on the wall. She was beautiful and just what he had needed to find his redemption. His life was good, but in this case, well, it had all the earmarks of something very sinister. He just had to keep Katy out of this.

Mike started to pick up the phone to call Katy at home and check on her doctor's appointment for that day, but he heard the ringer signaling the front door had opened. It was Dan and Paul.

Paul told Trisha he had to go see Mike Parsons at his office and his dad was going to pick him up. Trisha watched Dan and him leave and drive away. She picked up the phone and dialed her dad, Rich, to see if he had any apartments available for Linda. He said he did and would love to go with Trisha to see Linda and help by letting her look at a couple of his places. Rich said he would be there in thirty minutes.

Rich arrived at Trisha and Paul's place, walked up to the door and knocked. Trisha answered and they both went inside as she got her purse and keys. Rich noticed that Trisha was more unsettled in her appearance. She had always been particular about her looks, especially when she was going out. He, of course, found her change now strange, but shook it off knowing what she was going through.

"How's Paul doing?" he asked, wondering what calamity was making his daughter look so tired and disheveled.

"Not good, Dad. He's meeting with Mike Parsons, the private investigation company's attorney. It seems the cops here have an anonymous letter pointing to Paul as a possible suspect. I know I look terrible, but I've been upset and crying ever since they left."

"Look, honey, don't panic. Maybe Mike Parsons can help him. Don't jump to conclusions," Rich said, patting his daughter on the shoulder as he led her towards the door. "Let's try to forget about it for just a while and find a place for Linda. I have a couple that I think she might like."

"Okay, Dad. But I'm really worried this time. I never knew Paul to be anything but kind. But now, I'm starting to get scared."

"I know, sweetie, but let's go pick up Linda. By the way, you didn't say where she was staying."

"She's staying in a hotel out on Glenstone."

"Good. Let's forget about what we can't fix right now and fix Linda up with a place. Then we can go back to your house and wait for Paul to get back and maybe we can look into it further when we know what the police have. Right now, let's try to focus on your friend. I'm right here with you, dear."

They got in the car and drove to the hotel. Linda was waiting in the lobby. It had been a while but, as Linda got in the car, Rich recognized her right away.

"Linda, how good to see you! It's been a long time."

"Sure has, Mr. Dishman."

"Call me Rich. There are a couple places on the south side of Springfield I'd like you to see."

"That sounds nice, and, thanks, Rich, for taking me to look."

They drove down Republic Road and finally stopped at one of Rich's apartments. He got out, taking the key with him. They walked up to the front entrance and let both girls in.

"This is really nice," Linda said, walking around. The modern kitchen and living room were much better than what she lived in when she was in Kansas City. The bedrooms were spacious and the deck outside was large enough to accommodate a few guests. "I don't really think there is any need to look further," Linda said, looking at Rich and back to Trisha. "This will do just fine."

"Well, we do have some papers to sign," Rich said. "We can do that tomorrow at Trisha's house. You can move in any time after that. I'll even skip the first and last month's rent since you're a friend of Trisha's."

"Wow, thanks, Rich. Isn't that great, Trisha? Trisha? Where did she go?"

Just then the sliding glass door opened, and Trish came in from the deck, locking the door behind her. She had slipped out when Rich was showing the bedrooms to Linda.

"Nice view out there, Linda," Trisha said, looking back towards the doors.

"Well, your dad said I could have this one and skip the first and last month's rent."

"Well, he's very nice and the best dad ever." Trisha said, walking over to hug her dad.

"Reminds me of the place we stayed at in college, don't you think, Trish? You remember, the one over on West Sunset?"

Trisha stopped for a second. She seemed lost in thought.

"Oh, yeah, the one with the deck like this one?" Trish asked.

"Well, it didn't have a deck, Trisha, but I know that was a long time ago. That's when that cute guy who lived there used to come over and sit with us at the pool. You remember his name, right?"

"Stephen?"

"No, silly, it was Randy," Linda said, walking close to Trisha. "I wanted to jump his bones," she whispered near Trisha's ear.

Trisha just shook her head and smiled sheepishly.

"Well, let's get back," Rich said. "I'll get the papers ready and meet you at Trisha's place around nine am tomorrow. Trish needs to get back as she has some important stuff to look into."

Rich locked the door and they got into the car and headed back to Linda's motel. Linda leaned up from the back seat and whispered to Trisha, "Can't believe you don't remember Randy. He was hunky, and you wanted him as bad as I did."

"Shhh," Trish whispered back with a slight grin. Trish raised both eyebrows and put her finger to her lips. "That's our secret."

"What did you say, Trish?" Rich asked, looking over at her.

"Nothing, Dad. Nothing at all."

Trisha turned back and mouthed to Linda the words; "I have my hunk." They did not notice the car following them.

CHAPTER 27

Paul and his dad sat quietly as Mike entered the office. Mike walked around to his seat behind his desk. He looked each of them squarely in the eyes and instructed, "Look, if we are going to work as a team together, we have to be a team. There are no secrets, no hidden agendas, and certainly we stick together. In most cases in court, the truth and evidence usually win. That's why I'm here to ask some questions that need to be answered truthfully. We know the events that led up to this moment. Is there anything else you need to add, Paul?"

"I can't think of anything else. The night itself, well, it's just a blur but everything I told you was all I could remember," Paul said, putting both hands on the chair and sitting taller.

"Think hard, Paul. This is what I have to face later today and there are some things they may ask you don't need to answer. I will step in and say something like my client doesn't need to answer the question. So far you have not been charged with anything, so you should not answer anything related to the alleged crime or any kind of hypothetical questions they may ask. Just anything about where you live, what you do, and where you were that night is essential and you must answer that type of question, or they may hold you."

"I don't know what they would have besides the letter. Do you have any idea, Mike?"

"I don't. But let's not jump to any conclusions. We'll find out what they have later. I'll be the one to say when we are done answering questions. So far as we know, there is no body and there is no crime. Without a body, they will have a hard time proving anything. The less you say, the better off you are and that takes discipline. Don't allow them to anger you or upset you. You answer only questions I signal with a nod for you to answer, nothing else."

"Dan, is there anything else I should know?" Mike asked.

"Well, yes. The cop who wants to interview Paul is named Cory Blackwell. He worked on the case before with Paul that you know about. This is why I'm counting on you to keep Blackwell from making a case out of nothing and trying to get at Paul for losing his case last time."

"I see. I'll be careful to watch for that. I can see things from the prosecutor's side, so I should be able to recognize if there is something funny going on."

"Okay, Paul. It's time to head over. Unfortunately, Dan, it will have to be just Paul and me. I will get back to you when we are done. I will take Paul to his house when we're finished."

"Are you ready, Paul?"

"Yes, I'm ready."

Mike and Paul left the office and Dan went on to his car. He turned to look at Paul and Mike as they got into

Mike's car. Dan could not help but feel a strong sense of wanting to go and protect Paul. He was his father, and that's what fathers do. He never thought in a million years he would have had to ask Andy Marx for these favors. But here they were in their lives. Success just inches away for his son who had worked so hard to get there. Yet, Paul was inches away from losing it all. Dan was hoping Mike Parsons could be the guy to help Paul. The situation was becoming one wild thing after another. Dan got in his car and drove home. He really had no idea what crazy things were still in store.

Paul and Mike arrived at the police station ten minutes before the interview was to begin. Mike told Paul to be early was a sign of good faith and that as a witness, you wanted to be there. They walked inside and checked in. The front desk called for Officer Cory Blackwell to come to the front.

"Listen Paul, you are not a suspect as of yet. They are just questioning you as a witness or a person who may be in danger. You have to approach the interview that way. Remember to breathe, stay calm, and don't answer anything. Remember, you came here voluntarily and that counts for something. You are not required to answer anything except your name and address," Mike said, touching Paul's arm and looking him in the eye. A hallway door opened and Cory Blackwell appeared.

Mike studied Blackwell, who stood about six-foot with a well-proportioned body. He looked fit and was around thirty-something Mike guessed. His eyes were bright blue and his head shaved. Blackwell wasn't exactly muscular, but Mike figured he could handle himself. Mike didn't want to sell him short, especially if he had something against Paul. But Mike saw him immediately as cocky, and he had seen these guys before. Mike knew what approach Blackwell would take.

"Mr. Taylor, I'm Officer Cory Blackwell. I know we have met before. I just would like to ask you a few questions. Who is the gentleman with you?

"I'm Mike Parsons. I am representing Paul Taylor. I will be present during this session and during any and all questioning the department wants to do with Mr. Taylor."

Blackwell frowned, "Okay, follow me if you will."

They went through the same door Blackwell came out and stopped in front of interview room one. Blackwell opened the door and the three of them went inside.

"Mr. Taylor, Mr. Parsons, this is Detective Eddie Larson. Detective Larson was assigned as a special investigator in this case." Larson held out this hand to Mike and then to Paul as they shook hands and introduced themselves. Mike and Paul took seats at the table.

Mike studied Larson and wondered if he had any real connection to Blackwell or was this going to be routine and business-like. Mike could see the "good cop, bad cop" team sitting in front of Paul and him: Larson, the nice, soft talking guy, and Blackwell, the tough street cop.

Larson advised Paul of certain rights he had during the interview process. He stated that Paul had not been charged with any crime and was only being interviewed to see if Paul needed protection in the case. Larson made sure Paul understood his rights.

Larson leaned back in his chair and then leaned forward towards Paul and asked, "Can you please state your name and address?"

Paul looked over at Mike and he shook his head in the affirmative to answer that question. "My name is Paul Taylor and I live at 520 Pine Meadows Drive in Redfield, Missouri."

"Mr. Taylor, the reason you are here is that the department received an anonymous letter stating that you may have been possibly involved in a crime. We are interviewing you for your safety as well as investigating this accusation thoroughly."

Mike and Paul made no comment.

"The letter also states that you may know where a dead body is hidden and if we want to know, we should ask you. Is there any reason at all that you would know anything about those comments?" Larson asked.

Again, Paul looked at Mike for help. Mike shook his head in the negative.

"No comment," was Paul's response.

Blackwell jumped in. "The person writing this anonymous letter seems pretty accurate about what they know and that something very sinister has taken place. Where were you on the 14th of April this spring?"

Mike rubbed his chin but gave no indication, so Paul responded with a "no comment" again.

The interview went on for about another ten minutes and the questions seemed targeted at Paul to raise either anger or defensiveness. They were not successful. With each question, came a new "no comment" response, just as Mike had schooled him on back at Mike's office. Paul had held his tongue and was successful in not responding. Paul showed great patience, especially with Officer Blackwell, who seemed intent on drumming up something on Paul. So much so, that Mike began to worry that either Paul was a good client or that he was diabolical in some way. Mike had remembered past perps he had deposed who were almost as smooth as Paul had been in this interview. He quickly brushed the thought aside as he heard Larson break in.

"I think this interview has come to a close. It appears that you have chosen the right to remain silent. Would you like to sign a copy of the interview notes and what has taken place today?" shoving his notes towards Paul.

"My client doesn't need to, nor will he, sign anything at this point," Mike broke in. "He has no legal obligation to do so."

"Very well, you are correct," Larson said, rising from his seat, facing Mike and Paul. "You will be released under investigation. That means you are not being charged with any crime, but I want to advise you that the investigation of the anonymous letter will continue. If you can think of anything you need to talk about or something happens that puts you in danger, please don't hesitate to give me a call," Larson said, as he extended his card towards Paul.

Mike reached in between Larson and Paul and intercepted the card and placed it in his file. "Thank you, Detective Larson. If you are not charging my client, then we have answered all the questions that we are going to answer today." He gave his own card back to Mr. Larson. "You may call me, with any questions that are to be directed to my client as long as he remains under any investigation and has not been charged. Good day, gentlemen."

With that, Mike and Paul got up to leave. Mike noticed the pursed lips on Cory Blackwell and how it made him seem like a petulant child that did not get his way. Mike made a mental note of that and would be cautious about this cop in the future. Larson seemed cool and distant and did not seem to be pressing. Larson had been here before, and he knew how to handle this kind of situation. After seeing how Blackwell treated Paul, Mike mentally included

Blackwell as a possibility of being a suspect, too. His actions and body language were giving things away about him. He needed to tell Andy.

They got in the car and headed back to Paul's house. It was quiet for a few minutes as Paul reflected on the last time he was questioned and how he thought cooperating and answering questions was the best thing to do. It didn't work out so well as the officers, Cory Blackwell included, used it all against him. He was lucky to have a good lawyer then, and he felt luckier to have Mike Parsons this time.

"You have any idea, Paul, who might have sent that letter?"

"No, not really. But I think it was whoever was trying to blackmail me. They are tired of not getting money from me, so they are going another route."

"You need to be very careful and watch your back," Mike suggested, as he drove onto Pine Meadows Drive. "You never know what lengths people will go to get what they want."

In a minute, they were in Paul's driveway. They sat and talked for a few more minutes as a set of eyes watched from the tree line near Paul's house. A set of eyes had watched him from there before.

Mike gave Paul some last instructions and reminded him to not share anything with Trisha. "You can blame that on me," Mike said, as he gave Paul one last bit of instructions. "You sit tight, Paul. You don't talk to anyone without talking to me. Especially anyone you suspect in this anonymous letter thing. You talk to Andy and me only. You can't even discuss this with your dad."

Paul nodded, "Thanks, Mike. I can't tell you how much I appreciate what you are doing for me."

"Look, go in and get some rest. Tell Trisha I'm handling everything and that you can't talk about it right now. It's going to be okay. I'm going back to talk to Andy and see what we can figure out. Something has to break soon."

Paul got out and walked towards his house. He turned once more to wave goodbye to Mike. The eyes of the person watched Paul go in the house and then picked up the phone and dialed.

CHAPTER 28

Linda arrived at Trisha's house the next day to sign papers for the apartment. Trish met her at the door; they hugged briefly and went to sit in the living room.

"Your house is beautiful," Linda said.

"Thanks, Linda. I just love living here. I can't wait until Paul and I get to share this place as a married couple!" Trisha exclaimed, her eyes lighting up. "Dad will be here shortly."

"So, is Paul home?" Linda asked, looking around and then back at Trisha. "I can't wait to meet him."

"Speak of the devil, here he comes now. Paul, this is my friend, Linda. We went to college together. She has been very anxious to meet you."

Paul extended his hand, but Linda got up off the sofa and hugged him. "Nice to meet you, Linda," Paul said, looking surprised at Trish.

Linda turned her head sideways and winked at Trisha, holding Paul closer than Trisha was really liking. Trisha rolled her eyes at this. "It's nice to finally meet you, too."

"I guess you're here to sign the papers for the new apartment. Trisha's dad keeps the apartments up nice. You'll like living in Springfield again."

"Yes, I can't wait to get started looking for a new job. Your house is beautiful as well, your fiancée is quite the beauty, too!" Linda said, with emphasis and a bit of glee.

"Well, thanks, I think the world of her."

Trisha smiled in a way that if Linda wasn't there, she would have had Paul ravish her body right there. "I think the world of this man, too."

The doorbell rang and Trisha opened the door to let her dad in.

"Hi, everyone," Rich said, as he carried the folder of papers into the dining room and set them on the table. "I hope everyone is well today... we'll get to the papers in a minute. I hope everything is going all right for you, Paul. It must have been a trying two days."

"Yes, everything is fine," Paul said, nodding towards Linda and mouthing to Rich, she doesn't know anything.

Rich shook his head and passed the awkward moment as he led the girls to the kitchen table so Linda could sign the papers. Paul got his keys and told everyone he was headed to the office. He made the cutting motion across his throat to Rich, just to remind him to say nothing more about his troubles. Rich nodded.

"Well, here we go, just a few things to tidy up in the paperwork before we sign the highlighted areas. Then we'll go over these," Rich stated, pushing the papers towards Linda.

Linda started signing the papers and brought up an incident from college. "Trish, you remember the time we climbed up on the roof of the dorm and slept up there all night? I'll never forget it. Dodging security cameras and finally getting up there. We showed the boys how to get up there. You remember, don't you? You remember what you told me?"

"Uh, no, I can't recall right now," Trisha said slowly.

"Oh, sure you can. Don't clam up now just because your dad's here."

"It was college and, well, that was a long time ago," Trish smiled at her dad. "Well, I don't remember."

"Trish, you said, 'where's the beer'?'"

"Oh, yeah. I remember."

"Remember which boy climbed up and joined us?"

"I, I, uh, seem to have forgotten," Trish said, frowning at her lack of recall.

"It was Randy, silly. You know the hunky guy from our college apartment days. You invited him."

"I did?" Trisha's frown was becoming more pronounced.

"You did. Hey, are you okay?" Linda said with genuine concern.

Rich had a look of concern as well. "Linda, we've had a couple of rough weeks around here. Trish is a bit tired."

"That's right," Trisha chimed in. "I've been worried about Paul and his business and that's all I seem to be able to think about."

Linda returned to signing the papers, and Trisha put her elbow on the table and put her palm against her forehead rubbing it.

"Trish, could you get me a cup of coffee?" Rich asked.

"Sure, Dad."

Trisha got up and went to the coffee pot and poured a cup for her dad. She returned and placed the cup down in front of Rich with her left hand. Rich noticed.

"I guess your wrist is still bothering you, Trish?" he asked.

"Oh, yeah, it hasn't gotten much better."

Linda finished signing the papers, and Trisha's mind was somewhere else.

Mike and Andy were going back to interview John Restor one more time. They weren't convinced about his story, and Andy was sure that there would be someone else they could interview that may have worked the night in question. Someone had to talk, and it appeared it wasn't going to be John Restor.

They were on Campbell, headed to Redfield to Lee Hamlin's restaurant. Mike dialed Paul's phone.

"Hi, Paul. This is Mike. Andy and I were wondering what you know about Lee Hamlin and John Restor. Can you tell me about their relationship?"

"Well, for one, we basically fired John Restor. My partners and I found that he was stealing money in bonuses and perks from the company. We had an independent auditor come in, and they found out how he did it. We settled with his attorney and instead of firing him and making it big news, he quietly resigned and went away."

"Well, now, Paul, it seems he's working for Lee Hamlin. We are going back to interview him and maybe Hamlin, if he is there," Mike said, poking Andy in the arm and raising his eyebrows, signaling he was getting something of significance.

"You think they are connected?" Paul questioned. "I didn't know John was working with Lee. No one said anything about it."

"It makes our investigation that much more interesting. Andy and I are going to interview them right now. We've done it once, but came up with nothing. Something about Restor makes us think he is hiding something. We weren't tough enough the first time. We're going in much harder after what you have said about Restor. From your story about John's forced exit, we can see a pattern, and he would be someone you would want to avoid at the moment if at all possible."

"Yeah, I see something beginning to take place, too. Now that I know Restor is involved, things are starting to buzz around in my head."

"Ours, too, Paul. Ours, too. Andy and I will get back to you as soon as we can. I'll give you a call when the interview is done. There's something very suspicious about Lee and John. We're getting much hotter on the trail. Talk later."

Mike hung up and looked across at Andy as they pulled into the parking lot of Lee's restaurant. "Partner, something is going on with these two. I think we are beginning to connect the dots to the puzzle. John and Lee have teamed up in some way to work against Paul. This is all starting to make sense. Both men have a motive, which is something we were missing. At least we have that. Now if we could find the body and/or the weapon, we'd have it made."

"Mike, one thing you have to do while we're in there is try to get someone working in the restaurant to agree to come to our office and talk to us. You're the charmer. Why don't you see if you can get one of the wait staff to visit with you while I talk to Lee and John in Lee's office? Drop a card and see if whoever you talk to will agree to talk to us. If they agree, they need to be confidential. Remind them of that. I'll keep Lee and John busy while you do that. Just ask if you can find out when they work. It's worth a try. If you get lucky and find one, we will have something to back up our theory."

"And what's that theory?" Mike questioned, as he looked over at Marx.

"I think we both have the hunch that Hamlin and Rector are involved, but to what extent we don't know. Two guys with a motive to hurt Paul are starting to smell fishy. I think we're starting to feel the things cops feel when they are getting close to the plot. We're starting to hold point, just like a good hunting dog, and the birds are starting to run through the grass trying to get away. We need to hold point."

Mike grinned and they both got out of the car and started walking towards the door of the restaurant. John saw them coming and rushed back to the back to warn Lee that the private investigators were back.

CHAPTER 29

"Lee, they're coming in again! Those investigators. You need to leave. I can take care of them."

"All right, but look, don't answer any questions, we've given them enough. Just be evasive and hold them off. I have someone I need to meet anyway. Someone that can really help us. It will take a little cash and that will have to come from our personal accounts. No checks or credit cards, only cash." Lee said with a look of worried concern. "Now hold them off for a while, and I'll meet with this guy."

Lee left the building out the back door as Mike and Marx came in the front. The hostess greeted them and asked if they wanted to sit at the bar or in the dining area. She smiled politely, and Mike thought he would start with her. She seemed to be the honest type.

Andy broke in, "Ma'am, I would like to talk with the manager. My name is Andy Marx; he knows me and here is my card." She started to walk towards the back when she saw John making his way towards them.

"Hello, Mr. Marx. I assume you want to talk to Lee. I'm afraid he is out for a bit. If you leave your card, I'll be glad to let him know you stopped by."

"Actually, I came by to talk to you," Marx lied, wanting to put John off balance.

"Well... please... come on back, although I think I've told you all I can remember," John said, trying to be evasive.

"I just have a few questions I didn't ask last time and a few that crossed my mind since then," Andy said, as he walked back with John to the office.

Mike turned to the young waitress. He felt a bit funny trying to get this twenty-something young lady to talk with him. He was married to his pretty, pregnant wife at home. Now he found himself trying to smile and act suave to get her to talk. Not something he should be doing, but this job and the adventures before with Andy, well, they were all much more dangerous. This should be much simpler, right? Or would it be?

"Hi, what's your name?" Mike asked, smiling and looking directly into her blue eyes.

"Well, my name is Wendy," she said blushing.

"Hi, Wendy, I'm Mike. My partner wants to meet with your manager for a bit. I was wondering. Do you work a lot of hours here?" Mike said, smiling again, just for effect.

"Oh, yeah," she smiled and continued, "I work at least forty hours every week."

Well, the smile still works. I caught her blush, but remember, it's just business.

"I see. Do you work the day shift or nights?"

"Mostly days, I have a young child at home, but sometimes I work nights when someone doesn't show up for their shift."

"Hmm... we are private investigators, and we really

would like to ask you a few questions. But not here. I have a card if you could just call us and set up a time to interview. We're just trying to protect someone and if you were here on April 14th, you might be able to help us."

"What's this about?" she asked, stepping in a little closer to Mike. He could smell her perfume, and she stood in a way that made him feel a bit like his old drinking days and flashbacks started to hit him. He shook them off quickly.

"Well, we can't tell you much, but the information we get could save someone's life. We will keep your name confidential. No one from here will know if you come to our office for an interview," Mike said with a short wink, causing her to smile and blush once more.

Damn, I hate myself, but we need this information.

"Okay, I'll come in. I'll call when I can get there. I'll be looking forward to seeing you then," she paused, looking down at the card, "Mr. Mike Parsons."

Mike swore she winked back at him, but he tried to tell himself that she blinked instead, but he couldn't talk himself out of what his eyes saw. She did wink at him. He couldn't. Not now.

—▲—

Andy looked John in the eyes. He could see a faint sign of some fear or concern that John was trying to hide. Restor was faking his at-ease posture, as he sat across the desk from Marx.

"Mr. Restor, it seems like you told us you left the night Lee Hamlin closed for you. I know you really don't have to answer this question, or give up any records, but would you mind if I looked at the work schedule from that night, the fourteenth of April?"

Restor calmly tapped his pen on the desk, trying to

remain calm and not answer too quickly. "I suppose that will be okay, Mr. Marx."

Restor went to his computer at a separate desk to pull up the schedule. He was moving his eyes back and forth across the screen. "Hmm... that's odd. I can't seem to find it. Looks like someone could have deleted it or took it out. It skips from the thirteenth to the fifteenth of April. Maybe I forgot to put it in that day," Restor said, still with a more studious than fearful look. "I wonder if we got hacked."

"Interesting," Marx replied, standing up from his seat and walking to Restor. It was time to apply more heat, and Restor would be no match for Marx.

"Look, there is some pretty strong evidence that something is wrong here." Marx moved into Restor's personal space to aid in pushing the discomfort he must be feeling. "It seems like both you and Lee Hamlin would have an incentive to get some type of revenge on Paul Taylor. Rumor has it you got canned from Paul's company, and you were taking money. Good reason to get at someone, I would think..." Marx let his words in the air float for several seconds before continuing... "Mr. Restor?"

Restor froze and said nothing for what seemed like ten seconds but then broke in. "I think you're making inferences here, Mr. Marx, and that could be dangerous for you. I've got friends and an attorney to make you pay for those kinds of accusations."

"You're not threatening me are you, John?" Marx asked, leaning in even closer, close enough he could smell Restor's fear. "I've got a really good partner out there in the front of your restaurant that happens to be an attorney, too. Your threats pose no problem to us. What you better be thinking about is how deep you want to dive into this mess. If you have done nothing wrong, then get out of it before you get in over your head. Your past will work against you. When the cops get involved, the questions will get a bit harder, Restor."

Restor pursed his lips and then said, "I think I'm done answering questions here."

"As you wish, sir. But when the police get involved, just remember things are going to get a lot rougher for you. If you change your mind, give me a call. We're watching."

Marx left the office and headed back to get Mike who was waiting at the front lobby of the restaurant. "Let's go, Mike. We'll talk in the car."

Mike gave a short wave to Wendy as they left. On the way to the car, they said nothing, and Mike couldn't help but recall his brief psychological seduction of the young waitress. He felt like a heel and thought it best not to tell Katy about that short scene in the restaurant. He could claim it was all in the line of duty and not reveal any of their conversation. But Mike was all in with Katy. There were no more secrets. He promised her. Andy and he needed one more witness to confirm where Lee Hamlin was on that night in April. Wendy could be the one they needed to put the cops onto both men. But how he managed to get her to cooperate was, well, like the old Mike Parsons.

The little man on my left shoulder said, "No, don't tell her, it will complicate things. Katy's pregnant and she doesn't need to hear about this. Then the little man on the right, the one who smelled temptation, replied, "No more secrets."

Lee drove as fast as he could to the abandoned Go Kart track outside Redfield. He saw the black and white vehicle, with the lights on top, parked where the cop said he would be. He drove right by the police vehicle and kept driving to the parking lot of the ballpark. There was a game going on and there were several cars in the lot. Lee parked his car and watched the officer get out of his police cruiser, strolling quietly by the fields where the games were in progress. The officer waved at some folks as he smiled warmly at the moms and dads watching their young kids play baseball.

Lee waited until he was far enough away and got out of his car. He walked over to the patrol car and placed an envelope in the car. Lee got back in his vehicle and drove away. He pulled into the parking lot back at the abandoned Go Kart track and waited. He soon saw the black and white cruiser coming, he pulled out in front of him and lights came on. The officer pulled Lee over.

"Did you get it?" Lee asked, after rolling down his window.

"Yeah, I got it. Thanks Look, when do you want this done?"

"In a couple of days will work. Can you do it at night?" Lee queried.

"No problem. I think it will be better then anyway. I know the area we're talking about pretty well. I'll take Restor with me in my vehicle. We'll look like two officers making a call," the officer responded.

"We're both sticking our necks out here. But, if we're going to pin this on Paul Taylor, we need to strictly follow the plan and stay on time. We must trust each other. Keep an eye on Restor. Not sure what he's all about. It seems like the private investigators are putting the pressure on him. We need to get Paul Taylor arrested, and the body is the key. Paul Taylor needs to go to jail."

The officer walked away from Lee's car and slowly got in his vehicle, all the while looking all around, looking for anyone who might be nearby. Lee drove away and the officer followed. At the light, Lee took a left turn and the officer went right. They would go their separate ways, for now anyway.

CHAPTER 30

As Andy and Mike drove back to the office, they had much to discuss. Andy and Mike felt like they were closing in on Lee Hamlin and John Restor.

"John remained calm, but there was a moment at the end where I laid some things out to him that shook him up," Andy began. "He's starting to realize we know more about him than he thinks. He got to a point where he didn't want to answer any more questions. That's when I think someone guilty knows they are about to be reeled in... when they begin the silent act."

"This is starting to feel like the old Branch case, Andy. Those times were dangerous, but something more is happening, and we better protect Paul and Trisha. This could be more dangerous for them, too. We're starting to get the adrenaline that comes from getting close to the rabbit."

Marx offered up more. "John is starting to get nervous, he acted cool for a while, but I called him out on his getting fired from Taylor's Brew House. I think he has a motive to team up with Hamlin. Hamlin keeps avoiding us like the plague."

"We need to get this interview done with the hostess. Her name is Wendy. She seemed curious and acted like the type that would help."

"Mike, we need that one witness to blow up their alibi. If she does that, then we really have to move on this. That may mean calling in the police before we or possibly someone else gets hurt. It's not a game anymore. They are feeling the heat that we are getting close. But as you remember, those moments are when you have to be the most careful."

Mike remembered. Every now and then, it brought him new nightmares. More importantly, he thought of his wife, Katy, and their child on the way. He had to be careful. He was going to be a dad. He would need to return home from work every day. "I know I will be. I have to be."

With all the papers signed, Rich had gone and the two girls, Trisha and Linda, were left alone.

Linda leaned forward and took Trisha's hand. "Do you want to tell me about what's going on with you?"

"I don't know what you mean."

"Trish, you haven't been the same since we met up again. Several times you seemed a million miles away. You haven't said much, but are Paul and you having troubles? You don't have to tell me, but I'd like to help, if I can."

Trish sighed deeply and tears sprang to her eyes. "Linda, a few weeks ago Paul was driving home from a business meeting and hit something." A few tears fell onto Trish's cheeks and she struggled to tell Linda the story without involving too much detail.

"Paul says he doesn't remember, for sure, what happened that night. He said he had been drinking at the meeting and probably should not have been driving. Suddenly a detour sign was in the road and Paul swerved the way it pointed. He was blinded by a flash of light, and he thought he saw a deer jump out. He hit something, a deer, a tree, or something. But now he's getting called down to the station because someone saw it happen, and they're saying it was a hit and run!" Pent up panic and frustration burst from Trisha, without any restraint.

They're saying... that... they're saying he killed someone and moved the body! I don't want to believe it, but what if it is true? What if I really am marrying a killer? I love him so much, but I don't know what to believe. Is there something wrong with Paul... too much drinking, having blackouts... a brain tumor? Is there something wrong with me that I didn't see earlier? Why wouldn't he remember murdering someone?"

"Oh, sweetie, do you really think Paul could have done anything like that?"

"I-uh-don't think so... but I'm starting to get scared. I don't want to doubt him," Trisha sobbed. "Everything is so confusing to me."

Linda got up from her seat at the table and went over to put her arm around Trisha and did her best to comfort the pitiful woman before her. Tears started forming in Linda's eyes. "It's okay, it's going to be okay," Linda said softly.

Trisha sobbed, "I can't lose him. He's worked so hard for everything we have. This has come at a terrible time in our lives. He's working with private investigators called M & M Investigators. They are hot on this case. I just hope they find something soon."

Linda eyed the card for M & M Private Investigators Trisha had put on the table. "Hang in there. Really sounds like someone is jealous of Paul. Of course, he has the business, the prettiest girl in Redfield, and his future is bright. Maybe it's just someone who wants to get money out of him. It sounds a bit dangerous and hard to believe. But Paul seems so nice. I just could never picture him being guilty of anything like that."

"But put yourself in my shoes, Linda. He could be that guy that just blacks out and can't remember things he has done. I'm so worried for Paul."

"Has he been aggressive towards you?"

"No, he would never do that. In fact, he's very kind to me. He's so lost in his thoughts lately. It's hard for me to know how to pull him out of this."

Linda got up from the table, "Look, Trish, you know where I'll be staying, and I am going to try and get things moved in the next couple of days." She said, as she deftly palmed the card on the table and stuck it in her pants pocket. "Call or come by if you need to talk. Maybe you can help me arrange things at the apartment when the movers come? Something to take your mind off what's going on."

"Okay, just give me a call when you want me to come over."

"I have to run... only a couple of more days, until I move," Linda said, as she brushed the hair from her eyes. She reached out to hug Trisha as they both walked to the doorway of Trisha's home. As they hugged, Trisha did not hug Linda back as hard as Linda was hugging her.

"It'll get better. I'll see you soon. Call me if you need me."

Trisha closed the door behind Linda, and she walked over to the living room window and watched Linda get in her Chevrolet Equinox and pull away.

Linda pulled the M & M card out of her back pocket and looked at it as she slowly drove away from Paul and Trisha's place. She made a mental note to herself that she would contact the first name on the card. She noticed the address and plugged it into her phone's driving app. She was going to head in that direction and talk to this... Andy Marx.

Linda laid the card on the front dash and passed a gravel road. As she drove past, two men in a vehicle pulled on the county road and followed her. She never noticed the car as she drove towards the address the voice on the GPS function of her phone gave to her. Linda's thoughts began to review what had been going on lately with Trisha.

I don't remember Trish being like this. She just doesn't seem to be herself. I know, I would probably feel the same, but there are a few things that make me suspicious of what she said. I wonder what these private investigators know. Not sure, but I think I might try to find out. Curiosity killed the cat, I know, but I want to help my friend, and I think she needs my help. I'll see if the investigators will talk to me.

Linda drove on and, in just a few miles, pulled into the parking lot of M & M Private Investigators. She got out of her Equinox and pulled the card from her pants pocket and looked for that name one more time. She saw the name, Andy Marx, on the card. She walked across the lot and smelled the odor of tar rising from the hot asphalt that paved the parking lot. She looked at the card one more time, and then opened the door to the office, stepping inside.

The two men watched from a distance as Linda entered the building. One of them picked up the cell that was ringing, while the other started viewing all the pictures he had taken. They had several pictures from following Linda Hastings.

"We're watching her now. She went inside M & M. That's not a good thing. I think things need to speed up."

"What you're telling me is that we need to step up the plan?" the voice on the phone replied.

"That's exactly what I'm telling you. It may have to be tomorrow. I don't think we can wait much longer. Things are happening and none of them are good. Well, she's talking to someone in there, and who knows what she's asking or telling."

"Got it. Tomorrow it is."

CHAPTER 31

Linda Hastings entered the office and met Katy at the front reception area. Trisha had told Linda enough about Paul's predicament, that Linda was now concerned about her friend, Trisha's behavior.

Linda walked up to the desk and addressed Katy. "I'd like to see one of the investigators, please."

"They both returned to the office a few minutes ago. I'll see if Andy is available. Can I say who would like to see Mr. Marx?"

"I'm Linda, Linda Hastings. Please let him know I am a friend of Trisha Dishman's."

Katy's expression showed recognition of Trisha's name as she got up quickly from her desk. "I'll see if he's available." She walked back down the corridor to Andy's office.

"Andy, there's a lady out here saying she's a friend of Trisha Dishman. She looks fidgety, like she may know something."

"What's her name?" Andy asked, sliding his chair

from in front of his file cabinet back to behind his desk.

"Linda Hastings."

"Funny, I haven't heard that name in this case. Send her back and I'll talk to her."

Katy walked back to the front desk. "You can come back and see Mr. Marx. He's the first door on the left. The door is open."

Linda walked past Katy and then into Andy's office. Katy was glad she wasn't there to see Mike. It was still early in Katy's pregnancy, and she didn't know why, but she had these feelings of not wanting to lose her attractiveness and soon her body would start changing. She pushed the thought out of her mind, even though at times, she still worried about keeping Mike.

Linda stood across from Andy as he got out of his seat to greet her. He extended his hand and introduced himself. "Please sit down, Ms. Hastings. I understand you are here because of Trisha Dishman. Katy said you're a friend of Trisha's."

"Yes, that's right. I'm here because she told me about the case and what is going on with Paul. She seems to be under a lot of pressure. I want to help her, and I want to tell you things I have been noticing lately."

"What kinds of things?"

"First of all, Trish has always been right-handed but now she uses her left hand all the time... she says she might have sprained the right. She's very nervous and distant. She gets lost in our conversations and can't seem to remember some of our simplest memories," Linda stated, fidgeting with her hands. "She just doesn't seem to be the same."

Andy wrote some things down on his legal pad. He looked up at Linda and noticed for an instant how pretty she was. He figured she was around thirty something. Very attractive and for the first time in quite some time, he felt an attraction to a woman. He quickly returned to his questions.

"Ms. Hastings, are you aware of anything Trisha has told you that we should know?"

"Well, she's acting so strange. For a moment, I thought maybe she was on something, but I quickly put that thought out of my mind. We've always been close."

"You know, Linda, I've dealt with a lot of people that were unsuspecting and ended up doing some crazy stuff. One of them used to be my partner on the force when I was in Milwaukee. So I can't rule anyone out at this time."

Linda frowned. "I know this is petty, but when we were in college, this boy always came over. We both liked him but neither one ended up with him. He was a fun person. But I asked if she remembered, and she looked like she didn't know what I was talking about. Just stared into the distance. She couldn't recall his name. He came over often and I was sure she would remember."

"That's strange," Marx replied, while still jotting notes down on his pad.

"Something else. When her dad and I were looking over the apartment, she was outside on the deck, talking to someone on the phone. I thought it was an odd time to be on the phone. I just assumed it was Paul."

Andy wrote a few more things and looked up into Linda's eyes. "Have you told me all you know? Am I missing something, anything?"

"No, we've just been good friends and I hate to see Paul and her having this huge problem. But the funny feeling I can't get over, is that she is hiding something. I know her pretty well and the fact that she has acted strangely, well... it makes me question her, at least in my mind. I was just hoping you could help."

"We're doing our best. Why don't you leave me your

address and phone number where we can get a hold of you? I'll be looking into a few things in the meantime."

Linda gave her address and phone and thanked Marx. She walked away back through the corridor and passed Katy on the way. Katy and Marx both watched her leave.

"You think she's pretty, don't you?" Katy asked.

"Well, yeah, I do," Marx said, looking flushed. "I'm going back to talk with Mike. This woman said some things that give me a bad gut feeling. I might need to visit with her again."

Katy looked at the legal pad with her address he had written down, "Well, of course, you will," Katy teased as she smiled while turning to walk away.

"It's not like that, Katy."

"Maybe not now, but maybe later?"

Marx smiled and shrugged. "Right now, it's work."

Marx turned to walk to Mike's office. Katy grinned and shook her head. She knew when there was a connection. She was thinking that maybe Marx had found someone. She knew from experience that attraction could very well happen at the first meeting, like the first time Mike Parsons walked into her bar.

Linda was glad she had gone to visit with the investigator, Andy Marx. The bonus, besides the relief she felt that Trish was getting help, was the investigator was good looking and single. Linda smiled at herself in the rear view mirror and pulled out of the parking lot heading toward her new place. Two men drove a few lengths behind Linda's car, keeping her in sight. They weren't going to lose this one!

Chapter 32

Andy walked into Mike's office. Mike was hunched over his notes and seemed to be more pensive than Andy had seen him for quite some time. Mike looked up as Andy walked into his office.

"Sit down, partner. Make yourself at home."

Andy pulled up a chair. "Mike, you seem much more intense at the moment. What's on your mind?"

"To tell you the truth, Andy, the interview at the police station was interesting. I felt Officer Blackwell was a little too aggressive in questioning. We didn't answer anything but name, address and phone, but his way of questioning left me wondering just why it is that Blackwell has it in for Paul. He seems to want to get him in the worst way. It wasn't so much what he asked, it was more his tone."

"Mike, do you remember that Paul and Dan told us he worked on Paul's last case? He could have been embarrassed not being able to make anything stick to Paul last time."

"That could be. It may be a hunch on my part, but I do not trust the guy. Nothing seems fair about Blackwell and I think he's a dirty cop. I think Blackwell may be going rogue."

"Wait a second, Mike. Sometimes cops have to do some slightly underhanded things to get at the truth, or they may never find it. I'm not defending Blackwell, but at the same time, don't paint him with a broad brush yet."

"Okay, partner. But it is a strong hunch of mine. You know I get those feelings, and many have come true in our past. Just be careful about him."

"Sure thing, Mike. Hey, on another note I had an interview with Trisha Dishman's friend, Linda Hastings, a few minutes ago. She told me some interesting things about Trisha's behavior. She thinks she seems more distant and detached as of late. She even said she considered that maybe Trisha was on drugs or something."

Mike raised his eyebrows, "That could be, but there is something about Trisha that is also strange and when Linda, her friend, says something about detachment, well, that was something I could see in her, too."

Andy replied, "Detachment means that maybe she is covering something along the way. Maybe trying to hide something she knows about this case? Who knows, but until we get some real evidence, we can suppose all we want to."

"Well, Andy, you have that right. I have a couple of things to discuss with Katy, so I'm wrapping up my day. I'm going to take this stuff home and go over this interview one more time."

"Okay, that's fine. But tell Katy when you get home, that I'm not sweet on Linda Hastings. I just met her today."

"Katy is pretty observant, Andy. Maybe she is onto

something. It's okay to say you are smitten," Mike said, laughing.

Andy smiled a smile Mike had not seen from Andy in a long while.

Mike thought *my grandma used to say there is a lid for every pot. Maybe Linda Hastings is Andy's lid?*

"A lid for every pot," Mike said out loud as Andy rose from his chair.

Andy gave Mike a strange look, "What?"

"Oh, nothing, nothing at all. I'll see you tomorrow."

Andy left the office. Mike was gathering his things and was sure that he had wrapped up his day. He put everything in his briefcase and started to leave his office. That's when Katy appeared in the door.

"There's a very pretty woman here to see you. Says her name is Wendy."

"Oh, okay. She's a potential witness in the case. She works over at Lee Hamlin's restaurant. I wanted to see if she would come in and vouch for the whereabouts of Hamlin and Restor that night. I will see her before we go home. Go ahead and send her back."

"Okay, Mike." Katy turned to walk out and then suddenly turned back to Mike. "Do you still think I'm pretty?"

The question caught Mike off-guard. "Of course, I do. I love you with all my heart and soul. You are carrying our child, and there is nothing more beautiful in the world."

Katy smiled, making Mike smile himself. "Thanks. I needed to hear that, Mike. You know, just one of those days."

"Love you," Mike said, blowing her a kiss. "Now send her in so we can go home, and I can give you some real kisses."

Wendy Hartman was dressed very nicely and smiled as she extended her hand to a man she met only recently. Mike was sure Katy was not going to like this.

"Good afternoon, Mr. Parsons. I'm Wendy, Wendy Hartman, the girl you met at Lee's restaurant. I was the hostess."

"Oh, yes, Wendy, thanks for coming in. I have a few questions for you. You know we are a private investigating firm and that you do not have to answer any questions and you are under no legal obligation to do so. Do you understand?"

Wendy paused, as she was looking at Parsons. Mike asked the questions again, causing her to snap out of her mini trance.

"Ms. Hartman, do you understand?"

"Oh, yes, of course. Go ahead and ask me anything," she said, smiling widely.

"Do you remember if on the night of April 14th you were working in Lee Hamlin's restaurant?"

"Yes, I was working that night. I keep a work calendar and I brought it with me today."

Bingo! Mike thought to himself. "May I see it?" She handed Mike the calendar and he noted on that date she was, in fact, working. He slid the calendar back to her across the desk.

"Do you remember if Mr. Restor was working that night as well?"

Wendy answered right away. "Yes, he was."

"Mr. Restor indicated to me that he left early that evening and was supposed to close. He also told me Lee closed for him that night. Did he leave early?"

"No," Wendy leaned in closer and laid her arms on the desk, folding her hands in front of her. "In fact, John was closing that night. I never saw Lee Hamlin that night. I remember asking John where he wanted the new menus stacked for the next shift."

"Are you sure of this?" Mike asked. "This is very important to our case."

"Very sure. I'm positive John was there all night."

"Okay, then, let me ask you this. Has Lee ever closed the restaurant for John to your knowledge?"

"No, I don't think Lee would do that. His ego wouldn't let that happen. But I have noticed those two having very strange conversations lately, you know, not really work conversations. They find a private table and talk quietly. They look around suspiciously like they don't want anyone to hear. Are they in some kind of trouble?"

"Not really," Mike lied. *They are the main suspects, but someone like Wendy Hartman doesn't need to know.* "In my questioning, I'm trying to keep some people safe. That's all."

"Are they in danger?" Wendy asked, looking a bit more serious.

"We are working on something. There is a lot I can't tell you. But for your own safety at the moment, please be aware of your surroundings. Make sure when you get in your car and go anywhere that you check all around you. Don't take any unnecessary chances."

"Well, okay. That's kind of scary."

"I didn't tell you that to scare you. I don't think you're the one in danger. Just try to act like nothing is going on at work. You see anything suspicious, give me a call. My number is on my card. Is there anything else you can remember or want to tell me?"

"I can't think of anything right now," Wendy replied, as she looked at his wedding ring. "I think I'll be going now."

She picked up his card and rose from her seat. She offered her hand in a shake and Mike took it. She clasped her hand over the top of his and held on. She looked him in the eye. "I hope I have helped in some way."

"Oh, trust me, you have, more than you know."

Wendy smiled a sly, sheepish smile and finally withdrew her hand from Mike's. "I hope you find what you're looking for. If you need me to answer more questions, here's my number." She spoke the number out loud, and Mike wrote it on his notepad, followed by the word, Wendy.

"Thank you, Wendy, I'll be in touch."

Wendy walked out of the office, and Mike heaved a slight sigh of relief. He had passed a test and he felt like his redemption was coming around full circle. He gathered up his things, including the notepad and headed out the door. *I think I'm better. Yes, Katy, my Katy. That's what I have always needed. Someone I could actually fall in love with. And boy, do I love her.*

Mike walked to the front to get Katy so they could go home. He smiled at her when he saw the frown on her face. He knew what she was thinking. He wanted to make sure he reassured Katy when they got home, that his old drinking days were over, and that Katy was his one and only. His everything.

Chapter 33

Mike and Katy arrived home and Katy was in a pensive mood. They came into their home through the garage entrance and set their things down on the counter.

"Mike, can we go out and sit by the pool?"

"Sure, honey. Want something to drink?"

"I'll take a water, thanks."

Katy went outside to the pool area and sat in one of the poolside chairs. Mike grabbed two waters and walked out to sit by her. Mike leaned down and kissed her on the forehead and smiled, "You look wonderful in the light of early dusk."

"Do I? I feel like you've been so busy, we haven't gotten any alone time together to just think about us. The case seems to be taking up so much time."

"Well, we are getting closer to hitting something big. I can feel it."

"Mike, tell me something. What do you know about Paul's wife, Trisha?"

"According to Andy she seems lost and somewhat distant. Paul told him the same thing about her. Something about her has changed. Was acting differently towards him, although I'm not quite sure what he means."

"Do you think she would do anything bad to Paul? You know, like set him up or something?" Katy asked, taking a sip of her cold water.

"I'm not sure, but I'd give a hundred bucks to search that house. I think Marx is onto something and I think the answer is in that house. It's just a feeling I have. You know how I get those feelings."

"Yes, I do," Katy responded.

"That's what scares me. Whenever you get those feelings, it means some kind of terrible incident is about to take place. I told you in the beginning that I wondered about either or both of them having something to do with this. It was hard for me to determine if it was anyone else. But now, I'm worried about Lee Hamlin and possibly John Restor, the manager."

"So, you think that Paul and Trisha are innocent?"

Mike looked at Katy with a look of concern. "I didn't say that. I just said that these two guys may be guilty and are worth a hard look."

"Mike, something else is bothering me. Now that I'm pregnant, you do think I'm still pretty, don't you?"

"Of course, my love, the prettiest Irish lass on the planet."

"That girl that came in today. Um... Wendy? She was very pretty, too."

"I see where you're going and let me remind you of something. No one on this earth can do anything to pull us apart. You are my whole world and without you I might not even be here today. You're my rock."

"I love you, Mike. I could never be without you."

"You won't ever have to be. There is no one else for me. Just you, always you. Forever you. Now, I'm going to make a call to Paul. I think I'm going to ask him if we can get in the garage and look around in there. It needs to be a time when Trisha and Paul are gone. If they both have nothing to hide, they will let us."

Katy sighed and said, "Okay, but don't be long. I have waited all day to have you to myself. And I don't want to wait much longer."

"Okay, love, I'll make that call and I'm all yours."

―――▲―――

Paul answered his phone. It was eight o'clock and he had experienced a long day at work. His head was pounding.

"Hello, this is Paul."

"Paul, this is Mike Parsons. Katy and I ... well I wanted to ask if I could go back to your house's garage and look for more evidence, if you and Trisha give us permission, of course. I want to get a visual of the outside and who could have been looking at you and from where. The woods by your house would be a good place, and I might want to look around in that area as well."

"Mike, let me ask Trisha first and call you back. I don't see any reason why she wouldn't agree. We have nothing to hide from you. Just give me a few minutes, and I'll call you back."

"Okay, sounds good, Paul."

Mike hung up and waited for the return call. He had worked on this case for many hours with Andy. There were no more money demands, which he found odd. Now he was beginning to feel that something was way off. Something was about to happen, just like he told Katy. His old fears began to surface.

Mike's phone rang and he answered and saw it was Paul calling back. "Yeah, Paul, Parsons here."

"Mike, this is Paul and I talked to Trisha. She said she had no problem with you guys coming out. The code on the garage is 1768 and Trisha said she would be going out with a friend tomorrow afternoon, so that would be a good time."

"Okay, sounds like a plan, my friend. I will keep you posted on what we are doing. This will be over soon. I am sensing that we are getting closer to solving this one. Based on some of our interviews, I see many more suspects popping up. Two things I want to reiterate to you. One, avoid Cory Blackwell. Two, stay clear of Lee Hamlin. Those two, and your ex-partner, John Restor, are giving me bad thoughts."

"You think Lee was the one trying to get money from me?" Paul asked.

"Not sure but it makes sense. Restor and he have a motive. Just stay clear of them."

"Got it," Paul said and hung up the phone. He walked back to the bedroom, where Trisha lay there, partially nude on the bed, she slid the covers off and bared her beautiful, naked skin. He made love to her passionately for a lengthy time. Trish was intense. It has been so different these past weeks. It was a sexual awakening for him and for her, exploring each other in ways they never had.

When they had finished, Paul spooned against her body and rubbed her back and shoulder blade area. He noticed that she had a mole... actually quite a large one that he'd never noticed before. He'd cuddled with her several times before and never noticed this mole.

Have I been that unaware of my fiancée's body before? I hadn't noticed this mole. I could have sworn it was never there. But then again, I have been working so hard on this deal; I could have been not noticing her enough and paying attention.

He rolled back over to his side of the bed, as Trisha was now fast asleep. Paul slipped out from the covers and went out to the kitchen and grabbed water from the fridge. He downed half the bottle as Trish had put him through the mill. He leaned on the counter and thought... *the mole... why haven't I seen it before. Did it just develop, or has it always been there? These past few months have made me crazy, but I hope it's not... the big C or something. I will ask her about it tomorrow morning.*

Mike went back to the bedroom and Katy was already under the covers. Mike quickly got undressed and brushed his teeth. He walked back in from the bathroom and slid his body next to Katy. He had missed this for several days; he was feeling the urge to make love to his wife, his beautiful wife, the one that redeemed him from a life of drunken stupors and crazy women. To his bride, he owed much, and he was ready to show her just how much he loved her.

They made love and the sparks flew between them again creating a fire that had been missing for a couple of weeks. They had climaxed together and fell into each other's arms, and Katy quickly fell into a deep and satisfied sleep. Mike was wide awake. The lovemaking was beautiful, and they both needed the release, both mentally and physically. Yet, Mike couldn't get that feeling he had off his mind. It was a feeling that somehow and some way he was heading into another crazy situation.

He got out of bed and went out to the screened in porch. He stared out the screen and thought back to the days of Andy Marx and him with one crazy bitch,

Allison Branch. *When is the thought of her going away? She haunts me, probably haunts Katy, too. It was guns, explosions, knives, beatings, and kidnapping. These kinds of things don't happen to private investigators, do they? I thought all that action was for police and detectives. Just tell yourself this won't happen and that your gut feelings are wrong. And just when do we call the cops? We're starting to gather a lot of information about these guys. Maybe it's time to call them now.*

Mike wasn't sure how long he had been staring out of the screened in porch. He slowly turned around, and there she was. His skin tingled as he saw the gun pointed at him. It felt like every pore in his skin had a needle sticking inside. Mike couldn't move. He was frozen still, and he began to sweat. He started to put his arms out in front of him to reason with her.

But just as he did, Allison Branch disappeared. Like a ghost that haunted him, she had popped up in his dreams, in his thoughts, and sometimes while he dreamed on his feet, like now, while he was wide awake. But he didn't tell Katy he had these visions. He looked down at his feet and then back up only to meet a woman's eyes again. But this time it was Katy, asking him to come back to bed. They went back to the bedroom together, Mike's arm around his Katy.

Chapter 34

Lee stood staring at the old, rickety farmhouse. He had arrived just minutes ago and at this moment, all the things he endured as a child, all his crazy, demented thoughts, were pouring all over his tortured brain. He knew there was no going back on the plan. It was in motion, and the players had a job to do. All he could do was wait.

While he waited, Lee had to take one more look at the body. Being frozen, it was not the same. Her face would be disfigured from the beating, and it would be an ugly sight. But he did want to see it one more time.

He grabbed the key off the hook. Lee carefully undid the lock and slowly raised the lid to the freezer. The cold, frozen, ice-blue face stared back at him. The mangled face still seemed to exude terror. Being an awful human being, he was enjoying the sight.

Suddenly he thought he heard a car and quickly slammed the lid. He walked to the front of the old house, only to see a car passing by quickly. He couldn't make out what make of car it was, but it didn't look like anyone he knew. He let it go, stuck the freezer key in his pocket and went inside. He had things to prepare, as he was expecting company at the old farmhouse tonight.

Andy Marx had finally received the information he was looking for. He stared at the paper for quite some time. Marx had questioned Lee Hamlin all along, but the stunning information he was looking at, provided him with enough evidence to confirm in his mind what he had been thinking. Lee Hamlin owned the old farmhouse Trish had stared at so long the night Andy took them back to the scene. It was becoming clear to Marx. He was finally getting some breaks.

Marx quickly folded the paper and put it in his front pants pocket. He wanted to go back to the farmhouse and take a look for any clue leading to a body, a weapon, or any other clues that could help solve this case and put Paul Taylor and his fiancée, Trisha, in the clear.

He drove towards the farmhouse. When he got there, he slowed down and saw there was a car parked in the drive. He drove past the farmhouse and turned around about a mile down the road. He wanted to get a closer look at the vehicle and license plate. He wanted to turn back onto the county road, but a couple of grain trucks got in his way. Marx's vehicle moved slowly behind the grain trucks, creeping along. Marx tried to pass, but there were cars coming the other way. When he got around to pass the trucks and reached the farmhouse, he saw that the vehicle was gone.

Marx caught a glimpse of the car not really recognizing the brand but knew it was black. It was an SUV, and he couldn't quite see the brand from this distance. He saw the vehicle go over the top of the hill and when he reached the top, the vehicle was gone from Marx's sight.

He drove to the office and wanting to make sure he was reading the information correctly and draw some type of conclusion. He felt he had a very good idea of what was happening, but he needed the evidence. He needed a dead body. All the evidence and what he saw today was telling him there was a body somewhere on the property. Marx told himself he would go back after dark.

Marx entered his office and sat down. His first call was to Mike Parsons. "Mike, I've found some terribly disturbing information. I wanted to know if you could come meet me at the office and take a look."

"Well, we're at our doctor's appointment for Katy. I'll call you back in a few minutes."

Marx hung up. His information was telling, but he had to find a body or a weapon. All the motivation factors are here. Marx's phone buzzed.

"Yeah, Mike."

"Just got done with our appointment and heading to the car. What's going on?"

"I found out some information that will make you cringe," Marx said, as he paced around his desk in his office. "I'd really like you to come take a look at it."

"I'll take Katy by the house, and I'll come right over. I should be there in about fifteen or twenty minutes."

"Got it." Marx said and hung up.

All he could do for now was wait for Mike to come. He was sure of what he was thinking and when Mike got there, he could talk about what evidence he had and what his theory was. Marx stared back at the paper.

Of all the damn craziest things ever, this case might top them all. I needed a body. We needed some luck. I just can't believe what I am thinking. Surely what I'm thinking can't be right. Or can it? I need to check on Linda Hastings, too. Well, just to see how she's doing on her move into her new place.

Marx found the address on his legal pad, and he quickly put the address in his phone's GPS. He would pay her a visit a bit later. But for now, he was waiting on Mike.

Mike was driving, all the while telling Katy about Marx having some information he needed to look at. Katy frowned, knowing this new information may be the beginning of one scarier episode she knew all too well.

"You know, Mike, we are supposed to go by Paul's house. He told us we could go in and look. We need to be there and out before 8:00 this evening," Katy said, shifting slowly in her seat.

Mike responded while still paying attention to traffic. "Yeah, but we can stop by for just a few minutes. We just need to leave the house by six thirty. It's just going on five now."

Mike saw the flashing lights ahead, signaling trouble. There had been an accident and they would be held up for a while. Mike called Andy and used the speaker phone.

"Hell, we're stuck in traffic," Mike said. "We're going to be here for a while. Look, let's just get together after we're done scoping out Paul's place. We can all meet back at the office."

"Yeah, okay, Mike. But this information is going to knock your socks off. I have an idea and I may go visit Linda Hastings and check on her, maybe ask her a few more questions. I'm definitely going back to the farmhouse. Lee Hamlin owns it. There has to be something there."

The fact Andy would check on Linda made Katy grin and she mouthed the words, "new girlfriend?"

Mike and Katy were now totally at a standstill in traffic, and they would be there for a while. "Look, Andy, let's meet up around eight thirty this evening back at the office after we've explored Paul's house. Who knows what we will find? All of this may make more sense at some point, and we might be able to piece this all together."

"All right, sounds good. But I am going by Linda's first and may go back to the farmhouse, just to take a look after dark."

"See ya."

They both hung up and Mike looked over at Katy and mouthed the words, "new girlfriend."

They both laughed. Mike was stuck in traffic, and it was one of his pet peeves. But there was no one he'd rather be stuck in traffic with than his beautiful Katy, the mother of his first child. Even though he was a bit agitated, he reached over and kissed Katy on the lips. He stared at her for a few seconds. "I love you, forever."

She smiled and said to Mike, "I love you to the moon and back."

Mike Parsons felt whole again. Katy was feeling blessed.

Chapter 35

Paul called Trisha from work. He was busy today, and he knew Mike and Katy were coming over to check the house. He reminded Trish they would be there and she and Linda had plans.

"Hey, honey. I'll have to be at work until after nine tonight. I should be home around nine-thirty."

"I did call Linda and I told her I would pick her up around 5:30 and we would go get something to eat. I can't wait for you to get home. I will have a special surprise just for you tonight. So, don't be late."

Paul felt warm inside. He had enjoyed Trisha so much lately and, in fact, he felt as though he was falling even more deeply in love with her. He knew he had made the right decision to ask her to marry him.

"I won't be late, dear. I will never pass on some alone time with you! Soon this will all be over, and we will set our wedding date."

"See you tonight and like I said, hurry home."

Paul hung up and went back to work. This whole

thing, this dead body, interviews with the cops, and people trying to extort money had to be over soon. Paul was getting weary, and he knew Trisha was, too. He had to think positive thoughts, and maybe Mike and Marx would soon get to the bottom of it all. He hoped anyway.

He thought of being framed and how someone was trying to make him look like the killer. *Why can't I remember, why?*

Paul rubbed his temples. He felt tired and sick of all this. He had created what he thought to be a once in a lifetime opportunity and, now, well, now it seemed like it was about to fall apart. But there was something he had to remember. Something he was absolutely missing. The past few months had caused his blood pressure to rise, and for a young man like Paul, his health was concerning. This all had to end... soon.

Linda was almost finished getting ready for Trisha to pick her up for dinner. She picked out something nice. She chose a black, above the knee skirt and satin blouse. She looked at herself in the mirror. She wanted to know if she would ever find the right man, just like Trisha had found Paul. The thought of Andy Marx came to mind. He was a little older, but not by much. But he was so handsome. Surely, she could find out a little more about him. She sure wasn't finding any men in her own age range, so why not?

Linda smiled at herself in the mirror. She tossed her hair and made sure her lipstick was right. Linda was just a tad jealous of Trisha. It seemed she had found the right guy. Successful and handsome, Paul was what most girls were looking for; someone to love them, honor them, and cherish them, just like Paul did with

Trisha.

She sighed deeply and sprayed on just a bit of perfume. Not heavy, but just enough to be noticed. Her phone rang and she answered quickly.

"Hello, Linda. This is Andy Marx. I was wondering if I could stop by a little later this evening and ask you a few questions about some things I am finding out. It has to do with Trisha."

"Well, what did you find out?"

"I can't tell you right now. I'd rather discuss it with you in person. Would you mind if I stopped by for a visit? I have something to do around eight-thirty or nine. But I could come over after I get finished."

Linda was feeling giddy. Of course, she would let him come over. "Sure, Mr. Marx, I'm going out with Trisha for dinner. She's coming by at five thirty to pick me up for dinner. We should be back by then." Linda would use just a little more perfume when she got home from dinner.

"See you around nine-thirty."

"I'll be here, Mr. Marx."

"Please call me Andy."

"Okay, see you later, Andy."

Marx hung up. He thought of how he liked how Linda looked in his office the day he met her, confident and together. He remembered how he had questions to ask. He had professional things to do, but there was just something about Linda Hastings making her different from many others. Maybe it was maturity, maybe class, but he knew for sure he liked whatever it was drawing him to her.

Linda looked at herself in the mirror one more time. She liked what she saw more and more. Maybe this time, she thought to herself, maybe this guy is the one.

Trisha was just a little late, and Linda was about to call. A knock on her door made her put her phone down on the couch. She looked at herself just one more time before going to let Trisha in, but to her shock and surprise it wasn't Trisha. Two men stood there and the arm came up from the second man and the chloroform overtook her as she fell limp into the bigger man's arms.

Quickly, they handcuffed and gagged her. They set her up on the couch as she would come to consciousness soon. The two men sat and waited patiently for Linda to wake up. They had the plan and, so far, it was working.

Finally, after a while, Linda came to a conscious state and her look was one of terror and surprise. She tried to talk through the gag and was muttering unintelligible words.

"Calm down, we're here for a reason. You're going for a ride with us. Calmly. You are under arrest, and we need you to come along quietly. Do not resist, as that will just make it harder on you," the uniformed officer said, grinning. "Don't make this any harder than it needs to be."

Linda's eyes were bulging. She was scared beyond belief, and she just knew these were the people terrorizing Paul and Trisha. She was no investigator, but maybe this is what Andy wanted to talk about. *Oh my god, they are going to kill me, they'd kill all of them and this was how my life is going to end. I can't even call anyone. I'm helpless and just have to do what they say. I have to go along and hope for a miracle.*

"Now, just get up and we will walk you to the patrol car. Don't make a scene, or we'll just make it look like resisting arrest. You might just get hurt. You got it?" the cop asked.

Linda just nodded as she got to her feet, thinking she would vomit from the chloroform. They both led her by her arms. The cop picked up the phone and stuck it in his pocket. He was covering all the bases. Paul Taylor would be responsible for this death, too. He would make sure he set it up perfectly. The son of a bitch was going down.

Linda followed directions and as the sun was beginning to set, she was stuffed in the back of a patrol car, and she knew she wasn't under arrest, and she wouldn't be going to headquarters. She knew that for damn sure. She wasn't under arrest; she was in captivity.

Chapter 36

The farmhouse had one light on when they arrived with Linda in the back seat of the car. Cory Blackwell looked around before John Restor and he opened the door to the police cruiser and removed Linda from the car. Cory and John each had a hold of an arm of Linda's and guided her to the front door of the house. Linda's sense of sight was not there as she was blindfolded and gagged so she could not scream. She was as scared as she had ever been in her young life.

She walked up the rickety and creaking steps of the old house, taking each step slowly not knowing if she would trip and fall or step into some trap. She had no idea what they had in store for her or who she was going to meet.

They led her to a straight-backed wooden chair and sat her in it, binding her legs to the legs of the chair. Tears began to flow down her cheeks as she was trying to see her mother and father's faces, trying to recall all the good things they had done together. Linda knew her life was going to end here in this rickety place. Linda thought of Trish and Paul and was wondering what trouble they would be in for, too. Her instincts had been right, and something was wrong. There was going to be some type of mayhem. It was why she had gone to Andy Marx. Her instincts.

This guy, maybe he's the one. Now, after she had dressed perfectly for Andy's visit, she would never see the guy she thought might be "the one." It made her tears flow even more profusely. Nothing ever seemed to work out for Linda Hastings.

She heard the quiet, singular footsteps walking towards her. Click, clack, click, and clack, with a steady beat across the wooden floor, getting louder as the footsteps grew closer. She could feel hot alcohol-laced breath in her face and, suddenly, the blindfold was removed. The face in front of her was twisted and evil. It made Linda jump, but she could go nowhere with her legs tied to the chair. Leaning back away from him, the chair began to tip over backwards but was caught by the policeman in uniform.

"It's party time!" Lee Hamlin proclaimed. "We're so glad you could join us for the evening."

Linda tried to scream, but the gag muffled all her attempts.

"Now settle down, young lady. There's no need to be frightened. The police are here!"

Lee chuckled at this own joke, smiling broadly as a few beads of sweat began to form on his brow. He pulled the gun behind him from his waistband and turned the gun on Linda.

"We saw you go to the private investigators office. Andy Marx... I think his name is? What did you tell him, dear?" Lee said, looking like a circus clown, frowning with his mouth but smiling with his eyes.

Linda looked around the room, trying to find an avenue of escape. But her desperation only mounted, knowing this crazy man held a gun on her and a cop, obviously a bad cop, was guarding the front door. Linda was in deep trouble. Fear gripped her and wouldn't let go.

Lee nodded to Blackwell, "Pull the car around back. We don't want a cop car in the drive. Restor and I will keep an eye on little missy here.

Blackwell nodded and went out the front door to move the car. He came back inside and locked the front door.

―▲―

It was 6:30 and Mike and Katy had just walked in the door. Mike was going to call Andy, but they were running short on time. Katy and he quickly changed clothes and were out the door in fifteen minutes. Mike made sure he stuck the garage code in his pocket and Katy and he both walked to their garage and got into the car. They were headed to Paul Taylor's house to search for clues.

The drive seemed quite normal, and Mike was pensive about meeting with Andy later. "What information do you think Andy has for us, Katy?"

"Not sure, love. I know he has been working hard with people's background. It may have something to do with it."

"Yeah, probably something on Hamlin or Restor I would think. What do you think of Paul and Trisha? Do you think Hamlin is the guy we're looking for?"

"I don't really know," Katy responded. "I just have this eerie feeling we'll find out something tonight. Either from Andy or from our own search of the Taylor house."

"You think one or both of them are guilty?" Mike asked, turning to Katy.

"You know, doing what Marx did for a living, he may have seen more than us, for sure. He may have better instincts to know. But right now, Mike, I think this could be anyone, including the Paul and Trisha."

"Well, until we look into it further, we can't rule anyone out. It was always Andy's number one saying. He always said everyone is a suspect until proven otherwise. Most every time he was right, never giving up on any lead or any one person."

They arrived in the driveway and walked up to the garage door. Mike punched in the numbers 1768 and the door opened. Mike and Katy went on inside.

Andy had set out for the farmhouse, wanting to take one more look. He had information to give Mike and Katy, but he wanted to look around one more time, before they met back at the office. He believed neither of them would take very long, and they would be able to meet soon with much more information in hand.

Andy popped over the hill and arrived at the farmhouse. He went on past and the same car he had followed and lost was parked in front. There were lights warning Andy that maybe someone was in there. He aimed to find out. He couldn't pull into the driveway because it would alarm whoever was in there. Andy drove on to the turnaround road he had pulled into before and parked the car to the side of the gravel road. He got out and made his way on foot to the farmhouse.

Once on the property, he moved slowly around to the back, trying to see something from the windows. He saw no figures, but only shadows, as he was too far away from the windows. Someone was in there, and he had to get a better look. Andy moved deftly through the back yard and tried to see what was on the back porch. He inched closer to the porch and saw a freezer sitting out there. A small outdoor amber porch light lit the area as Andy moved in closer. He felt the cool air on his face and a brief chill went through him. He knew something was wrong. He felt it in his gut.

He stopped by the freezer. Why a freezer? This place had always looked abandoned, especially when they were all out there before and Trish had stared at the house. But the car was there before, it was there now. He knew someone or some clue he wanted was in there. Andy took one more step and his foot hit the freezer, popping the unlocked top slightly open. Out of curiosity, Andy opened the lid, and there was a frozen face staring at him making him jump slightly, a body, just what we have been looking for. *Damn, I knew it was Lee Hamlin.* He closed the lid quietly and took one more step, moving to his right. He accidently kicked an old milk can, and it fell over making a loud bang.

The bang startled Lee, and he waved the gun at Blackwell. "Go check the noise out. We don't want any intruders here. Go take care of business. Probably just some nosy kids. Run them off. You should be able to chase them away."

Blackwell was out of the door, and Lee began to question Linda again.

"So, young lady, what made you think going to the private investigators was going to help?" Lee questioned, taking a vial from his pocket and taking another snort of coke. "We have it all covered, and it's a no brainer. Yeah, we set up poor ole' Paul. We asked him for the money, but the stupid son of a bitch went to the private investigators instead. He could have gotten out of it if he would have just been compliant. He never knew it was me. Yeah, I put the body in the trunk, and I took the body out of there, too. But it will be so good to see him go down in flames."

"Now don't scream... I'm going to pull the gag off of you. Be good or I'll put a bullet in your pretty little head."

Lee slowly removed the gag, and Linda did nothing but tremble.

"Aww, is she s-s-scared of mean ole L-L-Lee? Maybe I can make you less scared." Lee said, as he began to stroke her hair.

Linda pulled her head away, and Lee slapped her hard across her face. Her head jerked hard to her right and blood formed on her lower lip. She began to cry.

"Come on, Lee," Restor pleaded. "Don't hit her; she didn't do anything to you."

Lee aimed the gun at Restor. "Y-You shut the h-h-hell up!" Lee bellowed. "I only h-h-hired you because I felt sorry for you. Gave you a place in my world and made you rich. You ungrateful b-bastard."

Lee fired, and the shot hit Restor dead square in the heart. Restor grabbed his chest and fell, blood oozing into a bright red pool near his body. Linda screamed, and Andy heard it. He started to move towards the house. Suddenly he heard footsteps behind him. A swift hard fist crunched the side of Andy's face and he tumbled to the ground, rolling away and gaining his feet again. Quickly, Andy's mind recovered, and he used his hand-to-hand combat knowledge to dispense his attacker. He dragged the body close to the fence, and he easily used the officer's own handcuffs to cuff him to the metal fence post nearby. Andy, being an ex-cop, knew where to look as he removed Blackwell's gun, other weapons, and ammunition. He left him by the post and moved towards the house. Andy called 911 and gave them the address and said he needed back up. Chief Ken Satterfield got the message and headed to the farmhouse with other police officers and ambulance on route.

With back-up on the way, Andy knew he couldn't wait much longer. He had heard the scream inside, and someone was in there hurt or maybe even dead. Marx had to get to a window and assess the situation. He came to the living room window and saw Linda, the girl who visited his office, tied to a chair and bleeding. Andy also saw John Restor, slumped on the floor lying in a pool of blood. He drew his gun and was headed to the back door. He would surprise whoever was holding Linda from behind. He had a good idea who was holding her. He knew someone was in there but going to the front door was too dangerous. He had to save Linda.

CHAPTER 37

Mike and Katy were looking around inside the garage for any clues leading to the person or people responsible for a dead body. They had found nothing of significance in the garage, so they headed up the steps to the door leading into the mudroom of Paul's beautiful home.

Once inside, Katy marveled at the spaciousness of Paul and Trisha's house. It was inviting, smart, and yet practical with many rooms upstairs and down. They moved cautiously as Mike felt his gun nestled in the waistband of his pants. He kept reaching back for assurance that it was still there.

"There has to be something around here," Mike said, as he looked around in the kitchen drawers and cabinets. "There's not much I see so far."

Katy answered, "Maybe the bedroom. Seems like most people keep their secret things they want no one to see there?"

"Could be. Let's go have a look."

They both stepped into Paul and Trisha's bedroom and Katy saw some very sexy lingerie hanging on the bathroom door. She pointed to them, "Hey, this could be fun, what do you think? Would you like me to find some things like this?" Katy teased. "Looks like they have a little spice in their life."

"Hey c'mon, this is serious stuff, right?" Mike smiled, as he looked at Katy and then winked. "Well, maybe it would be after all."

Mike was going through the drawers and found nothing, and they walked down the hall to a second bedroom. There was a desk in there with papers strewn along the top. The room appeared to be used as a small home office. Mike moved in closer and shuffled through the papers.

"Hey, Katy, come here for a second."

Katy was admiring the paintings on the wall and Paul's awards stacked on the wall shelves of the spare room. Mike's request brought her back to the task at hand. Katy walked over and stood next to Mike.

"What is it, Mike?"

"A lot of nothing, except this one envelope. Says it's from a company that does the family ancestry. I can't find the information that was attached."

"There, Mike. On the floor, is that it?"

Mike picked up the papers and began to read it as Katy also read it over his shoulder. He stared at the words, but they seemed to stun him as he looked back and forth to Katy as she read along.

"Well, well, well, if it's not the two snoops? I suppose you just found out what you wanted to know, right?" Trisha asked, as she pointed her gun at Katy and Mike.

Mike slowly tried to go for the gun in his back waistband.

"Easy there, Parsons. You don't want me accidentally shooting your pregnant wife now, do you? Just slowly remove your gun and drop it to the floor. Then kick it over to me."

Katy looked at Mike, scared as she was once again in another predicament; the kind she thought was far behind her. Mike took the gun from his waistband and did as he was told.

"Look, Trisha. I thought you guys knew we were coming by to look. We told Paul. I was sure he told you. He said you would be gone. Just, just, don't hurt Katy. You can keep me as a hostage, but let Katy go."

"You are joking, right? You seem pretty dumb for an attorney. I'm not Trisha. I mean, you couldn't figure it out, could you? I'm Trinity, Trisha's identical twin sister. You know the one Trisha never knew she had. Well, I found out months ago when I did my ancestry search. You know how adopted kids always think they came from somewhere wonderful, and it was all a mistake. What a cruel twist of fate! Trisha gets the life I should have had, and I get a shithole like the Hamlins. Well, Trisha had the same idea to check apparently and the letter and information came today, addressed to Trisha, and you seem to have it in your hand, along with the rest of the information. Now why don't you just hand that to me before I get angry and shoot your pretty, pregnant wife?"

Katy looked at Mike in shock, and he returned with his own surprised look. *This is the information Marx had for them. Dumb luck kept us from seeing it before we came here. If not for that wreck in front of us, we would have known. Where is Marx? We need the cops here; surely, they will get here. They better hurry!*

Mike handed the letter over, and Trinity didn't get too close to Mike as she grabbed it. Mike and Katy were in deep trouble.

Chapter 38

Andy opened the back door that was luckily unlocked. He could hear a man talking, almost yelling as he slid next to the kitchen wall, trying to peek around the corner. The room was dimly lit, but he could make out Lee Hamlin holding Linda Hastings around the neck, with the gun pointed at the side of her head.

Marx slid around the corner and pointed his gun directly at Lee Hamlin. Marx only had one chance and that was to break Lee down and make him commit an error.

"Let her go. She hasn't done anything." Marx said, keeping his gun pointed at his subject.

"Well, h-h-here's our n-nosy private detective. Y-you know I'll sh-sh-shoot her," Lee said, sweat beginning to pour from his forehead.

Marx had seen criminals on coke before, and this one was classic. Andy had to be careful, or Lee could shoot her by accident, just from being that fidgety. Lee was seemingly out of control, his face contorted, and he was desperate.

"Look, there is a simple way out of this, Hamlin. It doesn't have to end this way. I know your past was tough, but don't hurt a young lady that was not involved in your past. She wasn't the one, it was your father, and he was the one, right?"

"You d-d-don't know anything about my f-father. You're just a nosy ex-cop that's about t-t-to get a girl k-k-killed."

"Like you killed that one in the freezer outside? How did you do it, Lee?"

Lee began to panic. He could feel the lock and key to the freezer in his pocket. *You left it unlocked, stupid. Yeah s-s-stupid, just like your dad always said. D-d damn it!*

"I d-d-didn't do that," Lee stammered. "That was P-P-Paul Taylor, and you know it."

"Paul didn't kill anyone, Lee. You did. You killed his wife, Trisha. Put her in the freezer outside. That is after you put the body in the trunk for Paul to see. Then you took the body out. You and that John Restor. Jealous of Paul, weren't you? I figured out your plan when I went back to your school records. It said you had a foster sister that left home. Well, your foster sister just happened to be the perfect one to fill in for his dead wife, since it was her twin. It wasn't hard to go back in records to find what I suspected. Twins born to a mother that didn't want them. Trisha and Trinity. Trisha Dishman got adopted and Trinity Davis was in foster care with you and your family, Lee."

"Shut up about T-T-Trinity. Sh-sh-she suffered under the old man, just like me."

"School counselor said she left because of you, Lee. That you abused her. It wasn't the old man that made her leave, it was you. You know she was going to turn on you, right? If she had turned you in, she would have had Paul, the house, and the money. No one would have known the difference."

Lee was backing up and slowly edging towards the front door. His grip was tightening on Linda's neck as her face was red. Linda's eyes were fearful. She knew if she left the house with Lee, and Andy was shot by Lee, she would be dead soon after. She had to do something.

Linda quickly shouted, "Shoot him, Marx. Don't worry about me, shoot him."

"I'll kill her, I s-s-swear!" Lee shouted, the coke gripping him harder.

"Your dad was right, Lee. What a screw up you are. You don't have the guts to kill her. You couldn't kill the old man, what makes you think you can kill her? You're going to blow it. The big plan to take over the Paul Taylor world; the one you couldn't make yourself. Just let Paul build the business, you slip in your foster sister, Trisha's twin, put the murder on Paul and then you and Trinity share the financial rewards when Paul goes to jail." Marx said, stepping a few more feet towards Lee. "But you didn't think of Trinity turning on you, did you?"

"Stay there, don't come any closer."

"You're a coward, Lee. Just like your dad said."

Suddenly, a voice behind Lee boomed, "Drop it!"

Lee, by instinct, released Linda and spun to face the voice. The cop fired and shot Lee Hamlin. Lee's eyes bulged and his mouth opened to scream, but no words came out of his open mouth. A hideous groan like an animal being wounded was all that was heard. With blood oozing from his head wound, Lee dropped instantly to the ground. Now completely free from the ghost of his old man, free from abuse, free from his stuttering and tortured mind, Lee Hamlin left the world as he had always known it... in a state of chaos.

Marx laid his gun on the floor and flashed his credentials for the cop, and then he went to Linda. The cop, Ken Satterfield, asked, "Where's Blackwell?"

"I cuffed him to a post outside. He was in on this plan, and he came up behind me and slugged me. But we can get to all that later," Marx said, as he comforted Linda. "I think my partner is at Paul Taylor's house, and I think they might be in trouble. You've got to get people over there in a hurry," Andy said, letting the paramedics have Linda. Andy nodded to Linda to let her know to go ahead, and he told her they would talk later.

"What's the address?" Satterfield asked. Andy told him the address, and Satterfield radioed for cops to get to Paul's house.

Andy figured they were in trouble, and he would once again, be right. It was up to Mike and Katy to survive, just like they had before. Marx got to his car and drove fast towards Paul's house.

"So, how do you want things to be, Mr. Parsons? You've got this pretty little wifey here, all pregnant and such. You have this nice little life and a kid on the way. Maybe you'll have twins, just like my mom had Trisha and me, never to be together as she didn't want either of us. She let me go and those horrible people put me in foster care with those animals, the Hamlin family. The old man was a drunk and my foster brother, Lee, well, he was such a pervert. But he did have a plan and got in touch with me. All I had to do was substitute and fill in for Paul Taylor's girlfriend, my sister! How twisted, right? But the money, hell, the money was too good, and when I found out my sister was in the dough, I just had to have her life for myself. I even had sex with him. My sister would be turning like a top in her grave if she knew." Trinity chuckled. "That's not so twisted, is it? I mean, after all the bullshit I went through, I deserved it, right? The handsome man, the big house, and all the money I ever dreamed I could have. Plus turning on Lee, well that will be the most fun, don't you think? Lee, going down for the murder, which he did do, Paul and I together in a beautiful life I could only dream about."

Katy winced at the thought, wondering if she and Mike were going to survive this time. She wondered if Paul would ever know the truth. They were once again at an incredible disadvantage with another terrible person holding them captive. Katy wished Marx would show up and take this villain out. But Katy was stronger now and she broke in. "Look, don't shoot us, you can leave now and get away. You won't be caught, and we can go on with our lives."

"You really think I'm stupid? You think I'd give up Paul Taylor and all that money?" Trinity asked, turning her attention to Katy. "You're the only witnesses left. I get rid of you two, and then I'm in the clear. Lee already took Trisha's friend, Linda, and the cop that picked her up is in on it with us. There is no way they will find any of you, and you won't find Trisha either. We had to kill her to make the plan work. You know, the dead body you're looking for. The one in the back of Paul's car? It's hidden in a perfect place and so will you two be hidden after I'm done with you. Then, turning the others in will be so easy. The new Trisha, the beautiful, sexy Trisha, living in Paul Taylor's world. Ha, imagine that! I might not have had it so good when I was young, but man, did I hit the jackpot now."

Mike and Katy knew Trinity wasn't going to let them go. Trinity, with a gun on them and one in the waistband of her slacks, would make sure they knew who was in control.

"We're going for a little walk now; just do what you're told. You know you can't live through this, not after what I told you." Trinity motioned them to the garage door. Mike was trying to think on his feet. Something had to be done, or there would be a double homicide and he and Katy would be the victims. They moved slowly to the garage, and Trinity pushed the garage door opener switch, and the door slowly began to rise. Its creaking sound was the only noise to be heard in the still and starry night.

CHAPTER 39

Marx was speeding towards Paul Taylor's house. He called Paul and told him to stay away and that something bad was happening. He could fill him in later but Marx reminded him to please stay away.

Paul was at work and immediately got to his feet. He grabbed his car keys and, not heeding any of Marx's warnings, he headed for his house. He had to see if Trisha was all right. He drove eighty miles per hour and squealed his tires around the last curve and entered his road. He sped down the road and stopped in the driveway. He opened the garage door and entered through the side door.

When he got inside, he found nothing immediately. No one was there. He searched every room only to find rustled papers on the floor and the smell of women's perfume. Someone was here. *I can smell it.* The fragrance is certainly Trisha's. Paul knew in his heart she was gone, taken away, but by whom? Just who was doing this to him? He thought of Lee, Restor, even someone he might not know, but the fact was, Trisha was gone. He had to find her.

Marx was speeding to the house. He saw Paul's car in the drive. Shit! I told him to stay away. Was Paul involved in all this? Just then Marx saw Paul coming out of the garage. He drew his gun and pointed it at Paul. "Stop right there. Get your hands up." Marx barked. Paul immediately threw up his hands.

"Paul, what are you doing? I thought I told you to stay away."

"I had to check on Trisha. I couldn't see her getting hurt over something that was my fault."

Was there anyone inside?"

"No, no one."

"It's not your fault, Paul. I can't explain now but, right now, you have to stay here. I hear the cops coming. Just answer their questions, and I'll be back. I think I know where they went. I know Mike and Katy are also with her. She's not who you think she is."

I'll call the cops and let them know you are here waiting in the drive and not to hurt you. When they get here, just keep your hands up and answer their questions. Let them know I went into these woods looking for them."

"But, Marx, wait. Let me go with you."

"You just can't. It's too dangerous."

Marx disappeared into the woods to the side of Paul's house. Little did Marx know, Paul was hot on his heels.

Marx moved slowly and thought he could hear voices ahead. He tried to be careful not to disturb the ground floor and make noise. The air was damp and cool, and a light mist was starting to fall. The voices seemed to be getting closer; he could make out the one voice of his partner, Mike.

"Look you don't have to kill us. Look at my wife. You're a woman and you know what it means for a woman to be pregnant."

"That is what makes this my advantage. You're not going to do anything, or I would simply kill her and the baby without a second thought. But I'm going to kill you both anyway. You always knew I would because I can't leave any witnesses behind. I don't trust either of you to keep your mouth shut. Just like all the goody-goody kids in school. They couldn't wait to tell on ole Trinity Davis. So, I don't want you goody-goody people telling on me either. No, just turn around real slow."

Marx was close enough now, and hearing the last part of the conversation, it was now or never. Paul had made his way into the woods and he was near enough to see Marx raise his gun. Just then Paul stepped into the clearing. Marx yelled, "I said drop the gun!"

Suddenly, Paul began yelling at Trisha, "What are you doing? Have you lost your mind? What are you doing with a gun held on Mike and Katy? Things will work out, it's almost over."

"It sure is almost over. Paul, I'm not Trisha. I'm Trinity, Trisha's identical twin sister, who you knew nothing about. I was the one raised in the Hamlin house. I was the one taking abuse from my foster father and fighting off my predator of a foster brother. Why shouldn't I have what Trisha had?"

Paul stood speechless staring at the woman he had loved for years, or thought she was the woman. His head was going to explode with all the emotions and thoughts running through his brain, colliding and smashing everywhere.

"Lee and I took care of your precious Trisha! What a fool you've been! You made it so easy by being so wrapped up in yourself and your precious business. As long as we were having great sex, you never even questioned if something was different about me. How blind you've been!"

Suddenly, two shots rang out loud and clear. Trinity Davis slumped to the ground and so did his partner, Mike. Katy brought her arms in tight and shivered, then screamed. She felt nothing, but she knew Mike was hurt.

Marx kicked Trinity's gun away and attended to his partner, Mike.

"Hey, buddy, where are you hit? Her gun must have gone off when I shot her."

"My shoulder burns, but I'm not hurt badly." Katy rushed to Mike's side and began applying pressure to his wound.

Immediately, a police officer appeared and radioed for the first responders to give medical attention to Trinity and Mike. Marx asked the second officer on the scene to stay with Katy and make sure she was safe as she was expecting a baby.

"You're going to be fine, Mike. You officially have a war wound to talk about."

"Damn that was close, Marx. Can't you time things a bit quicker?"

"I did the best I could."

"Seriously, you did great. Thanks, my friend, for saving my life again."

"It's what we do, Mike. We solve crimes together."

Mike smiled through his gritted teeth as the medics loaded him on the stretcher and took him away.

Marx saw Paul drop to his knees and cradle

Trisha/Trinity in his arms. How could it be that Trisha had an identical twin, a mirror image? As he was holding her, he heard her whisper, "You'll never know how good it could have been. I fell in love with you." She stopped breathing and was gone.

Chapter 40

Two weeks later

They were all sitting in the offices of M & M Investigators, Mike, Andy, Katy, Dan, and, of course, Paul. They were recapping for Paul all that had taken place. Ever since Paul had found out that his dear Trisha had been the body in the trunk, he had been in a state of depression. He had to identify the body, which was a painful experience, find out the truth about the twins, and prepare for Trish's funeral. He had spent a lot of time with the Dishmans. They were devastated to not only have lost their only daughter, but that they would have to live with the guilt they had not even noticed the difference enough to figure it out. It was all a blur and the time went by so slowly. The big empty house was not the same without the love of his life. The smiling and loving Trisha was absent, and Paul kept realizing she was gone forever. His business had survived, but would he?

Marx began, "So, you see Paul, Lee was the one who killed Trisha and inserted Trinity in her place. That was easy for him to do the night you had your meeting. Lee was sick and should have had help long ago. But he went on to be jealous of your success. He wanted to bring you down, asking for the ransom money, making you think you didn't remember the crime."

"Right, Marx," Mike said, trying to add to the story. "Lee had a plan and it worked. It fooled us all until Andy found the school records for Trinity and Lee. They lived in a foster home, abused and neglected. Lee and Trinity parted ways until Lee came up with the plan to frame you, Paul. The thought of the money excited her. Thing is she would have gotten rid of Lee, too. If she could have killed everyone, she could have just stayed with you forever."

This gave Paul a chill, thinking back to the times he made love with Trinity, thinking it was Trisha and how wild she had been. *How could I have missed it?*

"But she didn't remember to get Marx," Mike went on. "She thought Lee was supposed to take care of that. Marx was ahead of Lee and had the information about Trinity already. Katy and I were supposed to get that information that night, but all hell broke loose. We got caught in a traffic jam, Marx went to the farmhouse, and we were caught in your house by Trinity."

Dan sat quietly, knowing what Paul was going through. He had been in his shoes before. He missed his dear wife like crazy, and he knew Paul would miss Trisha the same.

"So Restor and Blackwell had it in for me for different reasons? That's why they worked for Lee to execute his plan," Paul offered.

Andy cut in, "That's right, Paul. We used that information to track Restor back to the plan. But we didn't know about Blackwell until our meeting at the farmhouse where Linda was taken as a kidnap victim. Lee planned on killing her. Lee had everything in his favor until I accidentally found Trisha's body, and Lee sent Blackwell out to look for me. I didn't know for sure it was Trisha's body until later, but I had a pretty good idea it was her after I found out about the twins.

"I'm wondering why Trisha's parents didn't catch it," Dan asked.

"They did notice funny things about her, but Trisha always had an excuse. Like drinking coffee left-handed and not remembering things Linda knew from school," Marx added.

"I just can't think of why I couldn't see this," Paul said, shifting uneasily in his chair. "If anyone should have noticed more, it should've been me."

"You can't blame yourself, Paul," Mike added. "She was good at what she was doing, and she had time to think about it and how she would have to act, to be an authentic Trisha to you."

"Well, it doesn't make it any easier. I was fooled and too wrapped up in what I wanted for us. I was driven. I wanted my business to succeed more than anything. Now, I wish more than anything, that I had Trisha back. I would give my business world away to anyone if they could trade me Trisha for it."

"I know, Paul." Dan said. "I know exactly what you are feeling. Maybe it's time to go back to the house and just think things over a bit. I'm here for you," Dan said.

They all shook hands and the Taylors left together and walked out of the office door. It would be the last time they saw them in the office, but they would probably see Paul again at one of his restaurants soon.

They were all packed up for the day. Mike and Katy held hands and walked out of the office together. They were headed home and with a new baby on the way that was their excitement for now. Maybe now, they could get some much-needed rest and relaxation until the next case. They opened the door only to see the face of Linda Hastings.

"Hello, Linda, what brings you to M & M?"

"Andy Marx." She smiled a pretty smile as she went on back to his office.

Walking to the car, Mike turned to Katy and said, "New girlfriend."

Katy laughed, and Mike smiled back. Their world was getting back to normal.

Dan and Paul arrived back at Dan's home. Dan had invited Paul to have a cigar and a glass of bourbon on the back deck. They both sat quietly for a while, drinking their bourbon and blowing smoke into the early evening dusk. The lights were an orange hue across the sky, with the setting sun starting to go behind the clouds.

Dan took a long drag off his cigar and blew the smoke into the air as he had always done before. He could see his beautiful Rebecca and the long, curly, dark hair and gorgeous figure walking towards him, straight out of the smoke. This was an image Dan had seen many times.

Paul took a long drag off his cigar and blew the smoke into the air. He saw figures and images he could not make out at first. They were walking towards him. He saw blonde hair and green eyes. Paul took another sip of bourbon, thinking the images would go away. They were mirror images of each other. The twins, Trisha and Trinity, both had now appeared through the smoke. Paul blinked his eyes and when he looked again, only the image of Trisha remained. Trinity was gone forever.

Their mirror images were gone, only the love of his life remained. That was as it should be.

THE END

ABOUT THE AUTHOR

Born in St. Louis, Missouri, Malcolm Tanner was inspired to write by his high school English teacher. He spent thirty-four years in education as a teacher, coach, principal, and finally a superintendent. Sandy, his wife, and he retired to Table Rock Lake in Southwest Missouri. He says, "It provides a great backdrop and setting for thinking and writing." This is the fourth book in the Mike Parsons Series, and Tanner has started on the fifth. Malcolm has also written one stand-alone book, **Drowning My Suspicions**. The first two books are on audible, and he plans to do the others soon.

To find out more go to the following pages:

Facebook: (1) Malcolm Tanner LLC | Facebook

MT Followers Group Page: (1) MT Followers | Facebook

Instagram: Malcolm Tanner (@malcolmtanner8927) • Instagram photos and videos

Made in the USA
Monee, IL
14 April 2022